nt
you still don't remember?"
she said. "A Zug" – she pronounced the word with an intonation of hatred and disgust – "is a mutated ortholidan."

"That means nothing to me."

"An ortholidan is a monster. Some grow thirty feet long. They are flesh-eaters, very fierce, and the mutated ones are also very intelligent."

"What species do they belong to? Where are they found?"

"They belong to no Terrestrial species. As to where they are found—" She hesitated. "I can't tell you that yet."

"Why not?"

"You aren't ready. We thought you were, but we were mistaken."

"Ready for what? What do you want of me?"

She said slowly, "I'm going to be frank. We want you to kill a Zug. The Zug is in a certain place, very hard to get to. When you are ready, we'll take you there, then when you have killed it, we will reward you liberally." She smiled, showing small, separated white teeth.

BEYOND THE BARRIER

Damon Knight

Hamlyn Paperbacks

To SIDNEY COLEMAN
for mathematical and other favours

BEYOND THE BARRIER
ISBN 0 600 31460 X

First published in Great Britain 1964
by Victor Gollancz Ltd
First paperback publication 1966
by Corgi Books
Hamlyn Paperbacks edition 1978

A shorter version of this novel was published
in *The Magazine of*
Fantasy and Science Fiction
under the title "The Tree of Time"

Hamlyn Paperbacks are published by
The Hamlyn Publishing Group Ltd,
Astronaut House,
Feltham,
Middlesex, England

Printed and bound in Great Britain by
Hazell Watson & Viney Ltd,
Aylesbury, Bucks

I

The banked, fan-shaped classroom was silent with attention.

'And now,' said Professor Gordon Naismith, 'watch closely. I drop the charged particle into the tank.' He tripped the release of the mechanism suspended over the glass tank, and saw a silvery spicule drop, almost too quickly to follow, into the clear liquid.

'Contact with other partially charged molecules releases the time energy,' said Naismith, watching a sudden silvery cloud spread from the bottom of the tank, 'and, as you see—'

The silvery cloud grew rapidly, advancing on a wave front, a beautifully symmetrical curve that was determined by two factors: gravity, and the kinetic loss of the conversion process. It was perfect beauty, far beyond any curve of flesh or any line drawn by an artist, and Naismith watched it with a painful tightness in his throat, although he had seen it a hundred times before.

Now the change was complete. The tank was full of silvery fluid, opaque, mirror-bright and luminous. 'All the liquid has now been raised to a higher temporal energy level,' Naismith told the class, 'and is in the state you may have heard described as "quasi-matter". Tomorrow when we begin our experiments on this tank, we will see that it has some very odd physical properties. However, that concludes today's demonstration. Are there any questions?'

A student signaled with his desk light. Naismith glanced at the nameplate. 'Yes, Hinkel?' He stood beside the table on the dais, tall and big-framed in his laboratory smock, aware as he answered the students' questions that eight other Naismiths, in the other identical classrooms that radiated from a common center, were also standing, like eight mirror images of himself, also answering questions. It gave him an eerie shiver, just for a moment, to realize that he himself was one of the doppelgangers, not the 'real' Naismith – somehow that was almost impossible to accept, no matter how often one went through the experience ... then the moment passed, and he went on talking, calm, self-assured, his voice controlled and resonant.

The tone sounded, and the students began to stir, gathering their recording equipment and sliding out of their seats.

Naismith turned and fumbled for the duplicator control. The round brownish-black knob was hard to see, like a floating shadow on the table top. He found it at last, and turned it clockwise.

At once the half-empty classroom vanished. He was in the tiny, circular control room, alone except for the duplicator apparatus. His knees suddenly weak, he leaned against the demonstration table. Discordant memories swarmed through his head – nine sets of them, all at once, like interfering video broadcasts. It was hard to take, just for a moment, but after two years of it he was an experienced multiple-class teacher, and the nine sets of memories settled quickly into place in his mind.

As he prepared to leave, he became aware of an odd thing that had happened. The demonstration itself had been exactly the same in all nine classrooms, of course; it was only the questions afterward that had been different, and even those followed a familiar pattern.

But one of the students in – which was it? classroom 7 – had stepped up to the platform just as he was about to leave, and had said something extraordinary.

He stood still, trying to bring the memory into sharper focus. It was a dark-skinned girl who sat in the second row: Lall was her name, probably Indian, although it was odd that she sat apart from the whispering, giggling group of Indian girls, bright in their saris and gold earrings, who perched at the top of the classroom. She had looked up at him with her oddly disturbing amber eyes, and had said in a distinct voice: 'Professor, what is a Zug?'

Nonsensical question! It had nothing to do with the demonstration, or with temporal energy at all – in fact, he was sure there was no such word in the vocabulary of physics. And yet it was odd what a shock had gone through him at her words: as if, deep down in his subconscious, the question *did* mean something – and something vital. He could remember snapping to attention, all his senses taut, a cold sweat beading on his forehead....

And then what? What had he replied?

Nothing.

At that moment, the action of turning the control knob had been completed, and he had come out of the multiple state. Then the shock of reintegrating his consciousness, and now...

Zug.

The word had an unpleasant sound, somehow; it made a shudder of distaste run up his spine. Probably the girl was disturbed, that was all; he would put in a query to the college psychiatric office.

But as he left the control room, taking the rear stair to his office, the feeling of vague apprehension and unease lingered. Perhaps it was the strain of multiple-class work; not everyone could bear it. But he was proud of his ability to stand up under the load; he had never felt like this after a class.

He finished his day's record-keeping and left quickly, anxious to be out in the air. The afternoon was sunny and warm as he walked across the campus; he could hear the surf in the distance, and the Inglewood-Ventura monorail went hushing across, bright cream and tan against the blue sky.

Students were walking in little groups along the gravel paths between the flame trees. The lawns were richly green, neat and trim. The scene was familiar, soothing ... and not entirely real.

It depressed him to realize that after four years he still felt essentially disoriented. Everyone said he had made a remarkable recovery; he had passed his refresher courses with high marks, gotten his teaching license renewed: now he was established, competent ... and after all, these four years were all the memory he had: so why couldn't he settle down and feel at home?

Why should he feel there was some terrible secret buried in his past?

Irritated, he tried to shake off the mood, but the girl and her question kept coming back to the surface of his mind. It was ridiculous, and yet he couldn't help wondering if perhaps she had some connection with the lost thirty-one years of his life ... the blank, the emptiness that was his image of himself before the bomber crash that had almost killed him....

Zug...

Impulsively, he turned and took the path to the university library. There was a vacant information machine. He punched 'General', and then spelled out 'Z-U-G'.

The machine's transparency flashed, 'SEARCHING,' and then, after a second, 'GEOGRAPHY (EUROPA).' On the central screen appeared a portion of a page of text. Naismith read, 'Zug. (tsooK) 1. Canton, n. central Switzerland, area 92 square miles. Pop. 51,000. 2. Commune, its capital, on Lake of Zug S of Zurich; pop. 16,500.'

Naismith turned off the machine in disgust. Of course, he was wasting his time. It was a little surprising that there should be such a word at all; but the girl had said '*a* Zug', and besides, she hadn't pronounced it as if it were German. This couldn't be the answer.

As he was leaving the library, he heard his name called. Plump Mr. Ramsdell, the bursar, came hurrying toward him along the graveled path between the flame trees, holding out a parcel wrapped in white paper. 'How lucky to run into you like this,' Ramsdell panted. 'Someone left this at my office for you, and I absent-mindedly carried it out with me—' He laughed uncertainly. 'I was just going to take it over and drop it at the Science Building, when I saw you.'

Naismith took the parcel: it was unexpectedly heavy and hard inside the white paper. 'Thanks,' he said. 'Who left it for me, anyone I know?'

Ramsdell shrugged. 'Said his name was Churan. Short,

swarthy fellow, very polite. But I really wasn't paying attention. Well, I must fly.'

'Thanks again,' Naismith called after him, but the little bursar did not seem to hear.

Funny that he should have carried the parcel out of his office, straight to the library – almost too pat for coincidence, as if he had known Naismith would be there; but that was impossible.

Funny, too, that anybody should leave a parcel for him with Ramsdell; he had nothing to do with the bursar's office, except to collect his pay checks.

Naismith weighed the parcel in his hands, curiously. He had an impulse to open it immediately, but decided not to – problem of disposing of the wrappings, or else carrying them around. Besides, the thing in the parcel might be in more than one piece, awkward to carry unless wrapped. Better wait till he got it home and could examine it properly.

But what could it be? A piece of apparatus? He had several things on order, but was not expecting any of them immediately, and anyhow, when they did come, they would be delivered in the usual way, not left for him at the bursar's office....

Deep in thought, he walked to the tube entrance. He rode home with the thing on his knees, hard and metallically cool through the wrappings. There was no writing on the paper anywhere; it was neatly sealed with plastic tape.

The tube car sighed to a stop at the Beverly Hills station. Naismith went aboveground and walked the two blocks to his apartment.

When he opened the door, his visiphone was blinking red.

He put the parcel down and crossed the room with his heart suddenly hammering. He saw that the recorded-call telltale was lit, and touched the playback button.

A voice said urgently, 'Naismith, this is Dr. Wells. Please call me as soon as you get in; I want to see you.' The voice stopped; after a moment the mechanism clicked and the neutral machine voice added, 'Two thirty-five P.M.' The playback stopped, the telltale winked off.

Wells was the head of the college psychiatric office; Naismith went to him as a patient every two weeks. Two thirty-five this afternoon – that was when Naismith had been in the middle of his temporal energy demonstration. He had a sense that things were happening all around him – first the girl with her disturbing question, and the dark man leaving a package for him at the bursar's office, and—

At the thought, Naismith turned and looked at the package on the table. At least he could find out about that, and without delay. With a certain grimness, he seized the package, put it on his desk, and with a bronze letter opener began to cut the tape.

The wrapping came away easily. Naismith saw the gleam of blued metal, then spread the papers apart, and caught his breath.

The machine was beautiful.

It was box-shaped, with rounded edges and corners; all its lines flowed subtly and exactly into one another. On the top face there were oval inlays, arranged in a pattern that conveyed nothing to him, and slightly raised from the main shell. The metal was satiny and cool under his fingers. It looked machined, not stamped: fine, micrometrically exact work.

He turned it over, looking for a nameplate or a serial number stamped into the metal, but found nothing. There was no button, dial, or any other obvious way of turning the machine on. He could not see any way of opening it, except by removing the inlays from the top.

Naismith felt cautiously at the inlays, trying to see if they would depress or turn, but without result. He paused, baffled. After a moment, his fingers began tracing around the outlines of the machine: it was beautiful workmanship, a pleasure just to touch it – and yet it seemed without function, useless, meaningless....

Like the question: 'What is a Zug?'

Without warning, Naismith's heart began hammering again. He had an irrational feeling that he was being carefully hemmed in – trapped, for some unguessable purpose, and by persons unknown. His fingers left the machine, then gripped it fiercely again, pressing hard, twisting, trying to move some part of the mechanism.

He failed.

The visiphone blinked and *brrr*ed.

Naismith swore and hit the switch with his palm; the screen lighted up. It was Wells, with his iron-gray brush-cut and his deeply seamed face. 'Naismith!' he said sharply. 'I called before – did you get the message?'

'Yes – I just got in – I was about to vise you.'

'I'm sorry, Naismith, but I'm afraid this had better not wait. Come over to my private office.'

'Now?'

'Please.'

'All right, but what's it about?'

'I'll explain when you get here.' Wells' wide mouth closed firmly, and the screen went gray.

Wells' private office was a big, sunny room adjoining his home, with a view of the Santa Monica beach and the ocean. As the door slid open, Wells looked up from his desk, his big, leather-brown face serious and stern. 'Naismith,' he said without preamble, 'I'm told you insulted and frightened a Mr. Churan today. What about it?'

Naismith continued walking toward the desk. He sat down in the conical chair facing Wells, and planted his hands on his knees. 'In the first place,' he said, 'I'm not a criminal. Moderate your tone. In the second place, where do you get your information, and what makes you so positive it's correct?'

Wells blinked and leaned forward. 'Didn't you burst in on an importer named Churan, over in Hollywood, and threaten to kill him?'

'No, categorically, I did not. What time was I supposed to have done this?'

'Around two o'clock. And you didn't threaten him, or break anything in his office?'

'I never even heard of your Mr. Churan until today,' said

Naismith angrily. 'What else does he say I did?'

Wells sat back, put a pipe in his mouth and looked at him meditatively. 'Exactly where were you at two?'

'In my classrooms, giving a demonstration.'

'What kind of a demonstration?'

'Temporal energy.'

Wells picked up a gold pen in his big, well-kept fingers and made a note. 'At two?'

'Certainly. My afternoon class has been at two since March, when the schedules were changed.'

'That's right, I seem to remember now.' Wells frowned uncertainly, pulling at his lower lip. 'It's odd that Orvile didn't seem to know that, although I suppose it might have slipped his mind ... You know, Naismith, this could be a serious business. When Orvile called me, around two-thirty, he was shaking all over.' Orvile was the head of the Physics Department, a nervous, white-haired man. 'He'd just had a call from the police – this man Churan had complained to them, and naturally, he passed the buck to me. He knows I'm treating you for that amnesic condition of yours. Now, I'll put it on the line, Naismith – if you did black out and browbeat Churan, as he says you did, we've got to find out why.'

Naismith began to stiffen with anger. 'I've told you, I was in my classroom at two o'clock. You can check on that, if you don't choose to believe me – ask my students.'

Wells glanced at his notepad, scratched a couple of aimless lines, then looked up and said, 'You used the word "classrooms". I take it that means you were teaching by the multiple-class method.'

'That's right. Almost all the undergraduate classes are multiples. You know how crowded we are.'

'Surely. But what I'm getting at is this: at two o'clock you were in several places at once.'

'Nine places, or rather ten,' said Naismith. 'It's the nine-unit duplicator in the East Wing of the Science Building.'

'All right. My question is this: Is there any possibility that you were in eleven places at once, at two o'clock today?'

Naismith sat in silence, absorbing that. Then he said, 'Offhand, the idea is ridiculous. You say this Churan's office is in Hollywood. The duplicator field has a range of only about five hundred feet.'

'But would you say it's absolutely impossible?'

Naismith's wide jaw knotted. 'I couldn't say that, of course. Impractical, at least, in the present state of the art. What are you suggesting, that I somehow gimmicked that Hivert Duplicator to project one of my doppelgangers into a stranger's office?'

'I'm not suggesting anything.' Wells' pen made slow circles on the notepad. 'But Naismith, tell me this: why should this fellow Churan lie about it?'

'I don't know!' Naismith exploded. His hands clenched into powerful fists. 'Wells, something's going on that I don't understand and don't like. I'm completely in the dark now, but I promise you—'

He was interrupted by the *brrr* of the phone. Without looking away from Naismith, Wells reached over and touched the button. 'Yes?'

The first words swung his head around. 'Wells! Now see what's happened!' It was Orvile's shrill voice, and Naismith could see his white-haired head, grotesquely elongated in the visiphone. 'He's dead – horribly burned to death! And Naismith was the last man seen with him! My God, Wells! Why don't you—'

'Naismith is here in my office now,' Wells cut in. 'Who's dead? What are you talking about?'

'I'm telling you, Ramsdell! Ramsdell! My God, look here!' Orvile's paper-gray face withdrew, and after a moment the pickup tilted downward.

On the gray tile floor lay a plump body, sprawled like a hideously ruined doll. The head, chest and hands were nothing but shapeless masses of carbon.

'I'm sending the police!' Orvile's voice shrilled. 'Don't let him get away! Don't let him get away!'

2

With Orvile's hysterical voice still ringing in his ears, Naismith turned: in two quick strides he was at the door.

'What?' said Wells, slow to react. He half rose from his chair. 'Naismith, wait—'

Naismith did not reply. He slid the door open, whipped through, slammed it again behind him and was running down the walk. Blood raced warm in his arteries; he felt no fear, only an intense and almost pleasurable anger.

In the instant before Orvile finished speaking, the whole problem had become transparently simple. The police had no evidence against him in Ramsdell's death, and could not hold him; but they could, and would, delay him. And he was tigerishly convinced that his only safety now lay in striking back, as hard and as fast as he could.

At the foot of the hill, he caught a cruising municipal cab, and ordered the driver: 'Hollywood. I'll give you the address on the way.'

As the cab swung around and headed east on the Freeway, Naismith put a quarter into the phone slot and punched 'Directory, Hollywood'. The yellow transparency lighted up. Naismith punched 'C-H-U-R-A-N'.

The illuminated image jumped and blurred repeatedly; then it steadied on a page on fine print, slowly traveling past the scanner. Naismith punched the 'Hold' button. There it was: 'M. Churan, Imprtr', and an address on Sunset Boulevard. Naismith glanced at his wristwatch; it was just four o'clock, and most California businessmen did not close their doors till four-thirty. There was still time.

'This is it, mister,' said the driver, reaching over to turn off the meter. Naismith paid him and got out. The building was a yellow-stone monstrosity dating from the previous century. In the lobby, Churan's name was on the ancient white-letter directory. Naismith took the elevator to the fifth floor. The office, behind a corrugated glass door with Churan's name on it, was locked and silent.

Naismith rattled the door in a burst of anger. Raging, he banged the door back and forth in its quarter-inch of play, until the corridor rang with the sound.

The office next door opened and a pink young man stepped out, shirt-sleeved, with his necktie undone. 'Here,' he said. 'Here, what's the gas with you, son? Don't go like that.'

Naismith stared at him. The young man looked surprised, flinched, and stepped back into the shelter of his doorway. 'Nothing personal, son,' he added.

'Do you know Churan?' Naismith demanded.

'Sure, I know him, son – to say what ho. But he's gone, son – gone – zipped out half an hour ago. I saw him leave.'

Naismith stared at the locked door. He had been quick, but not quick enough. With an impatient surge, he put the full force of his arm and wrist against the doorknob: with a sharp ringing snap, the latch broke and the door swung in. 'Hey,' said the pink young man, his jaw open. 'Hey, now—'

Naismith strode into the reception room. There was nobody behind the desk, nobody in the inner office. Filing cabinets were standing open and empty; there was nothing in the desk drawers, nothing pinned to the wall. On one corner of the worn carpet, near the desk, there was a large, fresh ink-stain. There were some jagged pieces of glazed porcelain in the wastebasket, and a bedraggled bunch of yellow flowers.

Baffled, Naismith paused and sniffed the air. The office had an unmistakable atmosphere of vacancy; but to his sharpened senses there was a faint, jangling vibration in the room – yes, and a faint but distinct scent: something cold, musky and unpleasant.

When he left, the pink young man was still waiting in the corridor. Naismith said gently, 'What do you know about Churan?'

'Well, son, I never spread the air with him. Just what ho in the morning, way I told you. But he's a pro.'

'A what?'

'A professional, son. You know, show biz.' The pink young man pointed to his own open door, on which was lettered, 'REGAL THEATRICAL ENTERPRISES'.

Naismith scowled. 'Churan is an actor?'

'Got to be, son. He never got any parts through me, but I can tell. This importing piece must be a sideline. You looking for him real bad?'

'How can you tell he's an actor?'

'The makeup, son. Every time I see him, he's made up for the cameras. You might not notice, stereo makeup looks so natural, but I can tell. Every time I see him, he's got it on. Who should I tell him was asking?'

'Never mind,' said Naismith, suddenly depressed. He turned without another word and went away.

In his own doorway, in the act of withdrawing the key from the lock, he paused and stood still, listening. A prickle of uneasiness ran over his body. There was a smell in the air, a sickly, charred, greasy smell....

He went into the living room, through it to the bedroom. At first he saw nothing. Then, glancing at the floor behind the bed, he saw a woman's foot and a thick ankle. The smell was overpoweringly strong.

Sickened, he went around the end of the bed. On the floor lay a body he at first could not recognize, although he knew who it must be. Mrs. Becker, who cleaned his apartment on Thursdays – she was the only one other than himself who had a key. She was dead. Dead, and horribly burned. The face, chest, arms and hands were one shapeless, blackened ruin....

Naismith went numbly to the visiphone and vised the police.

They were there in less than ten minutes.

The cell door closed behind him with a sound of finality. Naismith sank down on the narrow bunk, with his head in his hands. The police had interrogated him for three hours. They had been very thorough; their questions had ranged from his private life, to his previous history and service record, his amnesia – how they had hammered at that! – to his work at the university, the duplication process, temporal energy, everything. They had even suggested the fantastic idea that he might have alibied himself in both killings by traveling in time.

'Temporal energy isn't available on that scale,' he had told them. 'You don't realize what prodigious forces are involved. Even with the two thousand megakline tau generator at the University, it takes several hours to charge the ninety liters of water we use in the demonstration.'

'But the water does move in time, doesn't it?' one of the detectives had demanded.

'Yes, but only a fraction of a microsecond, Lieutenant. The molecules are really only partly out of synch with our t.e. matrix. If there were a real displacement, they would simply vanish.'

The detectives would not give up. Wasn't it possible to develop the temporal energy process to a point where a man could travel in time?

'Possible, yes,' he had told them angrily. 'For someone thousands of years more advanced in science than we are. For us, now, it's a complete impossibility!'

Then they came back to Bursar Ramsdell. What grudge had he had against Ramsdell? 'None! I scarcely knew him!'

Then it was just a coincidence, was it, that Ramsdell had been murdered horribly just after being seen with Naismith? 'Yes!'

Guided by instinct, Naismith did not mention the parcel Ramsdell had given him. He could not explain the strength of the feeling to himself, but he was convinced that if he let the police take possession of the machine, a vital clue would be out of his hands.

Then his questioners turned to Churan, who had not appeared to identify Naismith, and could not be found. Had he murdered Churan, too, and hidden the body?

He patiently recounted what had happened at Churan's office, and named the pink young man as a witness.

Then what about the death of his housekeeper, Mrs. Becker – was that a coincidence, too?

Naismith grunted, clasping his head in his hands. How could it be coincidental that two people close to him had been killed in the same baffling way, within hours of each other? It was as if he were a sort of Typhoid Mary, an untouched carrier of disaster....

An idea came to him, and Naismith sat up straight. Erect and still, he was concentrating furiously when the outer cell door opened with a clang.

Startled, Naismith looked up. The jailer in his sweaty blue uniform was entering. He walked to Naismith's door, fitted a key to the lock, swung the door open. 'Okay, you can go,' he grunted.

Naismith stood up warily. 'I'm being released?'

'Your lawyer got you out on a writ. Come on, this way.'

'My lawyer? But—' Naismith fell silent and followed the jailer. Wells, when they had allowed Naismith to see him an hour before, had told him he would get a lawyer, but not to expect anything tonight. 'It's a first-degree murder charge,' the psychiatrist had said, 'and they won't release you on bail, I know. But I'll have Howard come down first thing in the morning. Be patient until then.'

Had he lost track of time – was it morning already? No, the wall clock in the jailer's office read 9.05 P.M.

'Here's your stuff,' the jailer said, tossing an envelope at him across the counter. 'Sign for it.'

Naismith scrawled his name, put the envelope in his pocket, and followed the jailer again. In the waiting room, a slender gray-haired man arose to meet them. He was dressed in a dinner jacket and carried a sleek pigskin briefcase.

'He's all yours,' said the jailer, and walked away.

'Mr. Howard?' Naismith said, advancing with his hand out.

'Eh? No, no. Jerome is the name; how do you do.' The gray-haired man shook Naismith's hand perfunctorily, then dropped it. He turned back his cuff to look at a wafer-thin wristwatch. 'My heavens, it's late. I didn't realize – although I must say the writ didn't take long. Well, anyhow, you're out. I really shouldn't have come down at all.' He paused, with a faintly bewildered expression on his pale face. 'Shouldn't have come at all,' he repeated.

They were descending the stone steps of the jail. Naismith said uneasily, 'Did Wells arrange with you about your fee?'

'Wells?' the other man echoed, looking abstracted. 'No, not Wells – I don't think I know him. You know,' he said, stopping again and facing Naismith, 'it's incredible that I came out tonight at all. I can't understand it. Why, I was at a dinner party. Good heavens, my daughter is getting married tomorrow—' His face twitched. 'Well, good night then,' he said abruptly, and turned away.

'Wait,' Naismith called after him. 'If it wasn't Wells who asked you to help me, then who?'

Jerome did not pause. 'Your friend Churan,' he said testily over his shoulder. His footsteps dwindled down the echoing walk. Presently he was gone.

Naismith woke up, aware that he was not alone in the room.

He had reached home close to midnight, dog-tired, and had fallen almost immediately into an exhausted sleep. Now he was wide awake in the darkness, sitting up, every sense alert to a warning of danger that crawled invisibly in the room.

There was no sound of movement; but the darkness was electric with the presence of something powerful and menacing.

Then, slowly, like a mirage in the air, a faint bluish glow came to life in the middle of the room.

Naismith caught his breath; the blue glow was continuing to grow slowly brighter, until now he could make out the squat shape of something hanging in mid-air.

It was a shape like a fat piece of tubing, bent downward to form an L. It was a gun, he saw now, as the light continued to grow: a pistol, clearly and unmistakably, although it was like no pistol that he had ever seen before. The thick handle was toward him, the barrel pointing away. Heavy and squat, the gun was a thing of subtle, powerful curves that melted into one another. Intuitively, he knew it was of the same family as the enigmatic machine Ramsdell had given him: completely different in form, they were still alike as brothers.

It hung there, unsupported, solid and real, and yet somehow spectral-looking in the blue light. It was bigger than any pistol made for a normal man's hand: Naismith could imagine himself getting out of bed, reaching out and taking the handle in his hand. And he knew that his grip would be barely big enough to hold it; his finger would barely reach far enough to press the trigger.

The silence was absolute. Naismith had forgotten to breathe.

The feeling of menace was still in the room, stronger than before, and it emanated partly from the weapon in the air, partly from the shadows beyond. The gun radiated a sense of brutal power: Naismith longed to touch it, and yet he was instinctively afraid of it – afraid of what ravening energies might be released if he touched the trigger. He knew, without any doubt or question, that the gun was no ordinary gun.

Then the darkness seemed to lift.

At the far side of the room, where his dresser and wardrobe should have been, Naismith saw a Something that stirred, with an impossibly fluid reptilian motion, and looked at him with tiny red eyes.

He was out of bed without knowing how he had left it, every muscle taut, the hair standing erect on his head.

The gun seemed to drift closer.

The darkness lifted still more, and Naismith saw the hideous, insect-reptilian form of the Thing, heard its armored plates grate together as it moved.

A thin voice suddenly whispered: *'The Zug! The Zug! Kill it! Take the gun – kill it, quick!'*

Naismith moved faster than he had ever done in his remembered life. With one hand he swept up the wooden chair beside his bed, swung it hard and let go. The chair crashed full into the suspended gun.

There was a sound like silk ripping, and a blinding flare of blue light that undulated across the walls and was gone. Half-blinded, heart hammering in his chest, Naismith found the wall switch and lighted the room.

The gun was gone. The Thing was gone. The chair lay smashed and blackened in the middle of the floor.

3

1. The Zug. [Twice underlined.]
2. Miss Lall.(?)
3. Things burned – Ramsdell, Mrs. Becker, the chair.
4. Churan. (?)
5. Ramsdell's machine, similar to gun.
6. Why did Churan accuse me, then get me out of jail?
7. Why???

Naismith stared at the list he had written. A pattern was forming in it, but it was maddeningly obscure. He rose from his desk and took a turn around the living room, moving nervously, combing his hair back with an impatient gesture. It was mid-morning: he had finally fallen asleep again toward dawn, and had slept until nearly ten.

He sat down at the desk again, staring at the list with narrowed eyes. The pattern ... He drew a light pencil line between Miss Lall's name and Churan's. The two of them, evidently connected, similar in origin ... one East Indian, the other, by the sound of the name, probably Iranian.... He felt a touch of uneasiness at this thought, but could not identify it, and went on. He remembered now that Miss Lall always sat alone in class; the other East Indian students invariably sat in close, gossiping groups. Did she avoid them because they would know she was not Indian, in spite of her name?

Why did Churan wear actor's makeup?

'Why, why, why . . .?

The pencil snapped between his fingers. Naismith sat back, deep in thought. He had done the one right thing last night, he knew intuitively, in hurling the chair at the spectral gun. Immediately afterward he had felt an overpowering sense of relief, almost of reprieve. But why? What would have happened if he had touched the gun?

He thought of the blackened chair, and shuddered. But he knew, somehow, that was not the answer.

He checked off the points on the list again, one by one. After a moment, hesitantly, he drew a doubtful line between 'Things burned' and 'Ramsdell's machine.'

Now the thought that had come to him last night in the jail cell began to take shape. Ramsdell had died after handing him the machine from Churan. Mrs. Becker had died after moving the machine from the desk to the closet. A common denominator: both had held it in their hands.

Naismith got up and went to the closet. The machine gleamed dully at him from the shelf. Reluctantly, he reached up and pulled it down. It lay heavy and solid in his hands; it was just heavy enough that, to hold it comfortably, an ordinary person would have to keep it at the level of his chest.

That was what Ramsdell and Mrs. Becker must have done. And they had been burned in the chest, face and arms – that is, in a radius of about a foot and a half from the point where they had held the machine.

If he was right, he had in his hands a thing of frightful power.

And yet he had held the machine, not once but several times, just as he was doing now.

Slowly he put the machine back on the closet shelf. He

returned to the desk, leaning over it and staring intently at the list.

The gun – similar in appearance to the first machine, and evidently wielding the same terrible power. He picked up the pencil, drew another line between the gun and the machine. Then he traced it again, making it heavier. *The gun had appeared after he brought the machine into the apartment.* There was one more connection: if he could trace them all, he would have the answer to the mystery.

He frowned at the last items, the questions of motive, then left them and went back to the head of the list.

The Zug. The word had a teeth-gritting unpleasantness for him now, remembering the shadowy creature he had seen in his bedroom last night. What was it? He had no more knowledge than before: but he knew in his viscera that it was real.

Miss Lall. There at least was a place to start. It was she who had begun the whole thing, with that abrupt question: 'What is a Zug?' Her voice ... was it similar to the one that had whispered to him out of emptiness last night? He could not remember: but he felt certain that Miss Lall knew more about what a Zug was than he did.

She had not asked because she wanted to know.

Why then? To start him thinking, to create a state of mind in which other things might happen ...? Naismith's fingers tightened on the broken stub of pencil. Yes, he wanted very much to meet Miss Lall again.

He thought briefly of taking the machine with him to the university laboratories, then dismissed the idea. It was too dangerous; he couldn't take the chance of injuring any more innocent people. Actually the thing ought to be in a vault by itself somewhere ... but barring that, it was as safe here as anywhere. He locked the door carefully behind him.

Youngsters were strolling on the shadowed campus lawns, oblivious as he went past them. Naismith called first at the Registrar's office. 'Dolly,' he said to the brown-haired woman at the desk, 'can you tell me something about a freshman named Lall – Samarantha Lall?'

The assistant registrar looked up, startled. 'Oh – Professor Naismith.' She hesitated. 'But, Professor, aren't you suspended? Professor Orvile said—' She stopped, embarrassed.

'It was all a terrible mistake, Dolly,' Naismith told her in a confidential tone. 'I had nothing to do with Ramsdell's death. They asked me a few questions and then released me. You can call up the police and verify that, if you like.'

'Oh, no,' she said, still looking doubtful. 'Well, I'm sure it's all right, then. What was the name?'

'Samarantha Lall.'

The woman turned to her files. 'Yes, here we are. Just a minute, I'll give you a stat of her card.' She dropped the oblong of plastic into a copying machine, handed the duplicate to Naismith.

Naismith examined the card. 'I see Thurmond has her in freshman English this morning.'

The woman glanced at the wall clock. 'Better hurry if you want to catch her there, Professor. That class is just letting out.'

Naismith thanked her hastily and left. He knew she would notify Orvile and there would be trouble – perhaps an expulsion. But he had no time for that now.

He saw her among a group of students scattering out of the main entrance of the Humanities Building. She stood composed and erect, in a dark blouse of figured silk and a short white skirt, with her books and equipment in her arms, waiting for him while he walked toward her.

Now that he observed her closely, she was an unusual-looking girl. Her skin was a dull tan, without gloss, even her prominent cheekbones. Her hair was black and dull. Her rather heavy features remained expressionless as he appoached, but her long, amber eyes regarded him with veiled amusement.

'Yes, Professor?' she said in her thin voice.

'Miss Lall.' He was fighting to control a sudden anger that made his hands tremble.

'Yes?' she repeated.

'*What is a Zug?*'

They stared at each other for a moment in silence. 'So you still don't remember?' she said. 'A Zug—' she pronounced the word with an intonation of hatred and disgust – 'is a mutated ortholidan.'

'That means nothing to me.'

'An ortholidan is a monster. Some grow thirty feet long. They are flesh-eaters, very fierce, and the mutated ones are also very intelligent.'

'What species do they belong to? Where are they found?'

'They belong to no Terrestrial species. As to where they are found—' She hesitated. 'I can't tell you that yet.'

'Why not?'

'You aren't ready. We thought you were, but we were mistaken.'

'Ready for what? What do you want of me?'

She said slowly, 'I'm going to be frank. We want you to kill a Zug. The Zug is in a certain place, very hard to get to. When you are ready, we'll take you there, then when you have killed it, we will reward you liberally.' She smiled, showing small, separated white teeth.

Oddly repelled, Naismith said, 'Then all this has been just to drive me into a position where I'd have to do what you wanted?'

'Yes.' She smiled again, and again Naismith felt a wave of repulsion.

'But why me?'

'Because you're a Shefth. Look—' She fumbled in her handbag. 'Catch this.' Her hand came up; something small and white hurtled toward him.

Naismith's left hand went out, caught the thing in mid-air, batted it violently away. It bounced on the grass and came to rest.

'You see?' she asked, a little shakily, staring at him with her luminous amber eyes. '*That's* why. Your reflexes are twice as fast as any – normal human being's.' She stopped. 'But I've said enough. Just one more word, Professor Naismith. Struggle against us. That's what we want. The more you struggle, the more ready you'll be. Now good-by.'

She turned away. Taut with anger, Naismith stepped after her, took her by the arm.

Her bare flesh burned cold into his palm. She was as cold as a lizard – or a corpse.

Naismith let go hastily. Her amber eyes stared coldly into his as she said again, 'Good-by, Professor Naismith.' Then she turned, and this time Naismith did not try to stop her. He watched until she disappeared around a curve of the flame-tree-bordered path.

After a moment his eye was caught by a glint of white on the lawn a few yards away. He went to it, stooped and picked it up. It was the object Miss Lall had tossed at him: a chrome tube like an oversized lipstick. He removed the cap gingerly: there was brown substance inside, the end apparently worn by use. On his thumb it left a brown smear, which would not come off, although he rubbed it vigorously with his handkerchief.

Turning the tube around, he saw lettering stamped into its side:

'WESTMORE CHARACTER SKINTONE NO 3: DARK SUNTAN.'

Naismith went home in a mood of suppressed fury. He pulled the machine down from the closet shelf again, set it on his kitchenette table, and stared at it while he ate a sandwich and drank coffee. The food satisfied his hunger, but his attention was not on it. He looked at the sleek, gleaming metal case as if by sheer force of staring he could penetrate its secrets. The metal was blue, like blued steel, but with iridescent glints of color. When he looked closely, he could just make out the fine paralleled lines of the machining. That was what gave it the iridescence, apparently. He examined the three oval inlays, tried again to turn or depress them, tried to force his fingernail into the cracks around them, but the separation was too fine. He turned the machine over, looking again for any joint, but there was none: except for the three inlays, the case was all one piece.

A prickle of uneasiness went up his spine. A machine is

incomplete without controls. This had none. Therefore it was incomplete: *the controls were elsewhere.*

Someone, out there, invisible ... sitting in a room, watching Naismith every moment ... with his finger on a button?

Naismith's fists clenched. The thing was dangerous, lethal; the fact that it came from Churan was proof enough that it was meant to work against him. And yet it was the only solid piece of evidence he had.

What else was there? He cast his mind back over the conversation with Miss Lall: all of it seemed subtly unpleasant now. Like an electric current, that cold touch of her arm had run back over all his memories of her.

After a moment he got up and took his notepad from the desk. Sitting again at the kitchenette table, he turned to the page where he had already listed what he knew about Lall and Churan, and wrote underneath: 'Shefth. Mutated ortholidan (sp.?). Not Terrestrial species.'

Under that again, he scrawled, 'Am *I*?' And immediately crossed it out with two heavy black lines.

He stood up, paced back and forth twice across the small room, then went with sudden decision to the visiphone and punched a number. To the university switchboard operator who answered, he said, 'Professor Sturges, please.'

'I'll see if he's available. The screen went gray, then blinked to life again. A pale young man peered myopically out of the screen. 'Bio office.'

'I'd like to talk to Professor Sturges, please.'

'Okay, I'll get him.' He disappeared from the screen, and Naismith heard his distant voice calling, 'Hey, Harry – run down and tell Prof Sturges there's a visi for him.'

After another wait, Sturges' cropped gray head and sallow, intelligent face came on the screen. Sturges held the Chair of Xenology; he was a quiet man, said to be well thought of in his field; Naismith had only met him once or twice, at faculty luncheons.

'Sturges, I need some information in your line, if you will.'

'Of course, but aren't you—' Sturges blinked at him with faint suspicion.

'It's all been cleared up. I'll explain when I see you,' said Naismith quickly. 'Meanwhile, what I chiefly want to know is this: according to my understanding, no intelligent humanoid race has ever been discovered off Earth. Is that correct?'

'Quite correct,' Sturges replied, still with reserve. 'In fact, no intelligent race at all. One or two are about as smart as a chimpanzee, according to the Europeans. Why?'

'A student of mine asked me to criticize an imaginative story of his,' Naismith said, improvising. 'Now this may be a little harder. Does the word "Shefth" mean anything to you?'

Sturges repeated it without interest, then shook his head slowly. 'No.'

'Zug?'

'No.'

'Have you ever heard of an organism called an ortholidan?'

'Never,' said Sturges succinctly. 'Is that all?'

Naismith hesitated. 'Yes, that's it. Thank you.'

'Any time,' said Sturges distantly, and broke the connection.

Naismith sat looking at the blank screen. He had been on the point of asking Sturges, 'Could a living human being be as cold to touch as a lizard?'

But he knew the answer. Reptiles and amphibia are cold to the touch because they have no self-regulating temperature mechanism. The temperature of warm-blooded animals varies between narrow limits; if it rises or falls beyond those limits, generally speaking, the animal dies.

But a cold-blooded animal's body temperature is always within a degree or two of the temperature of the air. And it had been cool and overcast this morning on the campus, when he met the Lall creature....

Naismith stood up, his muscles murderously taut. These people, whatever they were, knew more about him than he did himself. And that was intolerable.

'A Shefth,' he said aloud. The word still meant nothing to him, called up no image.

Where had he been, what unimaginable things had he done, during the thirty-one years that were blank in his memory?

Where on Earth . . . or off it?

Naismith thought frozenly, 'Everything depends on what action I take at this moment.' With every nerve alert, he could sense the gathering danger around him as if it were a visible, geometric web.

Suddenly he remembered the card the assistant registrar had given him, and took it out of his pocket. According to the schedule, Lall had no classes this afternoon. Her address was given as 1034 Colorada Avenue, Apt. C30, Santa Monica.

The tube took Naismith to within a block of the address he wanted – one of the old gray-stone apartment complexes, built during the Cold War, with deep shelters and storage vaults underneath. The 'C30' in Lall's address, he knew, meant that she lived in the third sub-basement of the converted shelters.

The foyer with its peeling plastic walls was empty. Naismith took the elevator down into a narrow corridor, poorly lighted, with numbered red doors at intervals. The ceiling was oppressively low; the floor was scuffed gray tile.

In a dead-end passage, he found the door marked 'C30'. A plastic card gummed to the door read 'Lall'.

Naismith paused, listening. There was no sound from beyond the door, and he had a sudden conviction that the apartment was empty. He pressed the buzzer.

The door clicked, swung wide.

In the opening stood Miss Lall, dressed as he had seen her that morning. Behind her he glimpsed a disordered, green-walled room. Cigarette smoke swirled up through the cone of yellow light projected by a lamp.

'Come in, Mr. Naismith,' the creature said, and moved aside.

Naismith's back muscles tightened. He stepped into the room, then paused.

Beyond a table, watching him with cold amber eyes, sat a brown-skinned man with a beard. After a moment, his resemblance to Lall was obvious.

Naismith walked forward. 'You are Churan,' he said.

'I am.'

Naismith said grimly, 'You sent me the machine. And you sent that lawyer to get me out of jail.'

'Thank me for that, at least,' the man said, narrowing his eyes. The table before him was littered with food and crumpled plastic. He picked up a chicken leg, gnawed it, spat out a piece of gristle. Scraps dribbled into his beard. He gazed up at Naismith with insolent eyes.

Lall came around and sat on the arm of a chair. Together, Naismith thought, they looked more inhuman than either alone. They were like two gigantic frogs, painted and dressed in human clothing.

A stir of revulsion went through him. 'Exactly what do you want from me?' he demanded.

'To begin with, why not sit down and talk reasonably together? What can be lost?'

Naismith hesitated, then sat in a leather chair facing the table. The room, he saw now, was cluttered with an astonishing number and variety of things. Books and papers were stacked unevenly on the floor, piled on tables. Naismith saw an icon, a bronze Chinese dragon, a plastic windup toy, a string of cheap green beads, a can of soup. Balls of paper and plastic had been tossed carelessly into corners. There were scraps of food on the floor. Dust was thick everywhere.

'What can we offer you in return for your cooperation, Mr. Naismith?' Churan asked. He picked up an orange, began to tear the skin off with his greasy fingers. 'Money?'

Naismith did not reply.

Knowledge?' Churan said delicately. Both aliens smiled.

Naismith leaned forward. 'Very well. You claim to know all about me. Let me hear some proof of that – give me details.'

Churan shook his head. 'Payment in advance, Mr. Naismith? Not a very good method of dealing.' He made a face, spoke a few guttural words to Lall.

'Doing business,' she said.

'Yes – doing business. We will not tell you everything now, Mr. Naismith. You have already learned something – that you are a Shefth, that the Lenlu Din sent you back—'

Lall interrupted him with a hissed word. He shrugged. 'Well, it does not matter. There is still much for you to learn.' He stuffed a segment of orange into his mouth and began to chew, blinking at Naismith in time with the motion of his jaw.

Naismith felt an unreasonable anger. He said, 'You're asking me to go into this blindly. Why should I trust you?'

Churan spat out a seed, stuffed another segment of orange in. With his mouth full, he asked, 'What other choice do you have?'

'I can refuse,' Naismith said. 'I can stay here, live out my life.'

'You are already under suspicion of murder,' Churan commented. 'You will lose your job—'

Naismith stood up.

'I am only stating facts, Mr. Naismith,' Churan said, staring up at him. 'If necessary, you will be convicted of murder and will receive a long prison sentence. We can even arrange for painful accidents to happen to you while in prison.'

Lall spoke to him warningly. He shrugged, and said, 'Only facts. Be realistic, Mr. Naismith – if you do not agree now, you will later.'

Naismith felt choked with anger. His voice was low. 'What if I kill you instead?'

Churan flinched. 'You will not,' he said hastily. 'But if you did, who would answer your questions?'

Naismith was silent. Churan's blunt forefinger stirred the papers on the table. 'Meanwhile, if you want proofs, I will give you some proofs. Look at this, Mr. Naismith.'

Naismith glanced down. Churan's fingers were spreading out a mare's nest of amateur-looking color photographs. Naismith recognized a dim picture of Fisherman's Wharf in San Francisco, a shot of the Neumann Obelisk in downtown

Los Angeles, a grinning closeup of Churan himself. Then something different came into view.

It was an oblong of what seemed to be clear plastic. In it were three tiny figures against a shadowy background.

The illusion of depth was so perfect that the figures seemed to be sunken beneath the surface of the table. Two were shorter than the other; and Naismith recognized Lall and Churan by their stance, even before he leaned near enough to make out the features. The third—

He stiffened incredulously. The third man was himself.

There was no mistake. Back in his apartment, Naismith took the photograph out of his pocket again and examined it for the third time. He had stared at it on the tube car going home, until the glances of other passengers had made him feel conspicuous.

There he was, embedded in the clear plastic, looking almost as if he might move or speak. Beside him, the two aliens gazed out with self-satisfied smiles.

'Where was this taken?' he had asked Churan. The alien had grinned up at him. 'Not *was* – *will be*, Mr. Naismith. You are going with us into the future, and this picture will be taken there. So you see, there is no point in argument.' He giggled, and after a moment Lall joined in. Their hoarse, grunting laughter was so unpleasant to Naismith that he pocketed the photograph and fled.

Now, staring at it again, he was compelled to believe. The background showed a room like none he had even seen before. The walls were paneled in magenta and ivory strips of some substance that looked hazy and blurred at the edges, although the rest of the picture was in sharp focus. There were chairs, tables of unfamiliar shapes.

He knew in his bones that the room was not of this place and time. Either he and the aliens had been together in the past, in that blank period that was the first thirty-one years of his life ... or else Churan had been telling the literal truth: this was a picture of something yet to happen – a snap-shot of the future.

If the aliens themselves could come back from the future into present time – if the gun he had seen in his room could be projected back – why not a photograph?

But if that were so, how could he possibly escape?

He ate a solitary dinner, went to a movie, but discovered after half an hour that he had no idea what he had been watching.

That night, he dreamed.

4

In the dream, he wakened to a sense of danger.

He struggled, gasping as he straightened his limbs. A thin mechanical voice was shrilling. 'Attack! Attack in the Fifth Sector! Guardians, awake! Attack! Attack!'

All around him in the big globular chamber, his comrades were rousing from sleep, squirming in the air, reaching for weapons. The automatic guns and other protective devices, floating at the outskirts of the chamber, ceaselessly revolved, their red lenses glowing.

The vision was so clear that Naismith accepted it without question. He had never really been Naismith; that was a dream. He was Dar of the Entertainer caste, and he was trying to get his wits about him. He had been on a thirty-hour patrol in the Eightieth Sector, and had barely fallen asleep, it seemed, before the robot alarm had wakened him.

His equipment drifted toward him as he grasped for it, half-blindly. He put on the helmet and plastron, seized the familiar shape of his flame rifle.

Other men were already pouring through the circular orifice of the doorway. 'Assemble! Assemble!' shrilled the mechanical voice. Still not thoroughly awake, he aimed his director at the doorway and followed.

In the huge assembly room outside, throngs of armed Entertainers were moving. 'Form squads!' another robot voice shrilled. Dar set his director to 'Group' and felt himself drifting across the chamber.

The whole mass of men was already in motion toward another open doorway. He recognized the men of his squad as they drifted together – Yed, Jatto, Opad. They exchanged glances and a few brief words. 'How many?' 'Don't know.' The words were not English, but he understood them.

Then they were moving across the room; the doorway loomed up. Tensing himself, Dar dived through.

Acrid smoke bit at his nostrils; clouds of it rolled down the green-lit corridor, so dense that he had to switch on his helmet ultravision. In the luminescent glow, he saw green-skinned bodies afloat, flesh torn apart, eyes staring blindly, mouths agape.

There was a thunderous roar from somewhere down the corridor. Dar felt something pluck at his arm, glanced down and saw blood welling. There was no pain, only a dull aching sensation.

A patrol officer came darting by. 'All over,' he said as he passed. 'We got them. Any wounded here?'

Dar signaled him, showing his pierced arm. The pain was beginning. The patrol officer signaled a robot, which cleaned his wound, extracted the sliver of metal, sprayed bandage on it.

'Dismiss,' someone was calling. 'Dismiss.' The men were crowding toward the doorway again, and Dar joined them. The press was so great that it was several minutes before he could go through. Grumbling voices sounded all around him. 'Waked us for nothing.' 'I'm going back to sleep.' 'No point to it – they'll just wake you up again.' 'Myself, I'm hungry.'

They were in the assembly room. Some dispersed through other doorways, but Dar's overwhelming need was for sleep. He passed through into the sleeping chamber, found himself a clear space, curled up in the air and lost consciousness almost at once.

Naismith awoke and sat up with a start. His heart was

hammering. His own familiar bedroom, in the darkness relieved only by the glow from the living room, seemed almost bizarre ... the dream had been so vivid.

He got up, turned on a light, stood blinking at his image in the mirror, then sat down on the bed. 'Dream' was not the word – he had *been* Dar. Looking back on it now, the experience had nothing of the incoherence or fantasy of a remembered dream. Every detail was clear and vivid, and as he thought about it now, he could even call up things that had been only hinted at in the dream itself.

The 'director', for example. Naismith absently stroked his left forearm. He could almost feel the shape of the thin, flexible device strapped to his arm. Whenever he wanted to move, in that curious place without gravity, he had merely had to tense his forearm slightly, and point in the direction he wanted to go.

That place *existed*. Sitting hunched on the bed in the predawn darkness, Naismith grimly strove to bring back all the details he could.

There were cloudy memories of dances performed in midair by troupes of Entertainers like himself ... a vision of a girl's face, and the name Liss-Yani. ... Naismith pinched the bridge of his nose between his fingers. The memories were fading.

Disturbed, he sat and smoked for half an hour before he went back to bed. Even then, he could not rest, and it was hours before he dropped into an uneasy sleep.

Sometime before dawn, he dreamed again of the staring, green faces of the dead men in the smoke-filled corridor. It was truly a dream this time, and he knew it; yet he could not shake off a feeling of horror as those hideous dead faces swam up toward him through the mist. They were silently trying to explain something; one in particular appeared again and again, face distorted, mouth agape. ...

Naismith awoke, with a confused sense that he had almost understood something important. At last, as he stood with razor in hand in front of the bathroom mirror, he realized what it was.

The face of the dead man, except for its green color and the lack of a beard, might have been Churan's.

It was Saturday; Naismith had nowhere to go, but the idea of staying in the apartment, even long enough to eat breakfast, was intolerable. He left the building and began walking up the curving street toward the park on the crest of the hill.

Suddenly and without surprise, he knew what he must do. He calculated rapidly: he had some four hundred-odd dollars in his checking account. That would be enough to take him to the East Coast, and allow him some breathing space to find a job until he could earn a teaching certificate in whatever state he chose....

His branch bank was only five blocks away. It would be better not to go back to the apartment at all.

The teller greeted him pleasantly. 'What can we do for you this morning, Mr. Naismith?'

'I'd like to close out my account. Can you tell me what the exact balance is?'

The teller's smile grew fixed. 'I don't quite understand, Mr. Naismith.'

Naismith scowled irritably. 'I want to close out my account,' he repeated.

'But, sir,' the teller said, 'don't you remember, you closed it out yesterday?'

'I *what*?' Naismith said, flushing with anger.

The teller's smile had vanished. 'Well, sir, if you'll wait just a moment, I'll get the records.'

He came back with a bundle of papers. 'Here is your closing statement, Mr. Naismith – we were just about to mail it to you. Here are your canceled checks – and here is your withdrawal slip, dated yesterday.'

Naismith stared at the paper. It was exactly what it seemed to be: a withdrawal form, made out for $412.72, and signed by himself.

'But this is a forgery,' he said at last, and stared at the teller. 'Who paid this out – was it you?'

The man blinked at him. 'I can't just recall,' he said vaguely, and turned. 'Oh, Mr. Robinson.'

The manager drifted over; he was a portly young man with a pale, dissatisfied face. 'Anything the matter?'

The teller explained it, adding, 'Mr Naismith claims the withdrawal slip is forged – but I know we paid it to him.'

'Well, I'm sure we can straighten this out. Howard, will you get on the phone to Jack Gerber and ask him to come over here?' To Naismith he said, 'Mr. Gerber is our attorney. While we're waiting for him, let's step into my office.'

Naismith crumpled the paper in his hand. 'Never mind,' he said abruptly. He turned and walked out.

He understood now what was happening; but understanding it made no difference to the wave of helpless anger that swept through him.

He was being pushed from one untenable position to another, like a king being driven by a series of checks across the chessboard.

Lall and Churan were making it impossible for him to leave Los Angeles, and impossible to stay. Under such pressure, how long could he hold out against them?

Back in the apartment, he realized abruptly that he still had one possible way out – the machine. If he could get it open, discover how it worked...

But when he opened the closet door, it was gone.

That night he dreamed again. He was afloat, in a crowded spherical room of pale green light. His own body was somewhere off in the darkness, lost in time and space: *here* was the City and the time was *now*.

'... only a few hours' sleep since the last attack,' the Dance Master was saying. His eyes were red-rimmed. 'However, it can't be helped. Assume formation for "Turbulent Wreaths". We enter at position 25, follow the silver for twenty-one and one-half spirals, and exit at position 32. Any questions?'

The others stirred in the air around him, beginning to form a long, slightly curved line aimed at the glowing disk of the doorway. 'What about afterward?' called one of the girls.

'Afterward,' said the Master grimly, 'we regroup for "Spheres and Fountains".' There were a few groans, but no protests.

The Dance Master came nearer. 'Dar,' he said in a low voice, 'how is your arm?'

Dar flexed his bicep. 'Better,' he said. 'It doesn't hurt.'

'I would have let you opt out,' said the Master, 'but there simply is not another man available. Do the best you can.'

Dar nodded. The Master hesitated, as if about to speak again, then went back to the head of the line. 'Ready,' came his voice.

The Entertainers faced each other, wiped their hands dry on their clothing, breathed deeply. A tone sounded. The Entertainers began to move, some gripping hands, revolving around each other, then letting go to dart ahead – the whole ensemble flowing forward in an intricate, graceful pattern.

Beyond the doorway, they emerged into a lighted sphere a hundred times the volume of the first one. As he went through his assigned movements, Dar was dimly aware of the crowded room whirling around him – the gaily costumed Lenlu Din, as raucous as a flight of parakeets; the robots drifting here and there, the greenskinned servants.

He gripped hands with the next man, whirled, released, twisted his body as he flowed forward around the silver streak of light. There was still no pain in his arm, but it was growing more and more awkward; once his grip failed, and he barely recovered.

The ensemble spiraled half across the room, past the little knot of dignitaries that clustered around the Highborn. Dar glimpsed her through the crowd – a fat, puffed little woman with mad eyes.

The room revolved again. 'Turbulent Wreaths' was a double-spiraled pattern, with a rolling movement that progressed along the line, checked, progressed again. It was not as difficult as it appeared, but when properly done it was pretty to watch.

Around once more. Dar felt a spasm of pain as he reached for his partner's hand. The man's eyes widened in horror; he reached quickly for his wrist, but Dar was already off balance, out of rhythm, the pattern broken.

Cursing under his breath, he spun in mid-air, put full power to his director and managed to slide into his place in the line. Somewhere off in the distance, a woman's voice was squawking indignantly. The Highborn – had she seen?

As they approached the exit doorway, a spindle-shaped robot drifted up, its yellow signal light blinking into Dar's eyes. Despairingly, he fell out of the pattern and watched as the rest of the line swirled through the doorway.

'Your name and designation?' the robot asked pleasantly.

'Dar-Yani, 108 class 3.'

'Thank you.' The robot revolved, tilted, drifted away.

Dar hung where he was for a moment, then thought of the marshaling room and dived through the doorway.

The others were waiting for him, pale and anxious. Their voices came at him all together: 'What happened?' 'Did he break the pattern?' 'What was the matter?'

'It wasn't his fault,' said Ten-Yani. 'I saw it. It was his arm.'

The Dance Master came forward. 'They say a robot stopped you. What did it want?'

'Just my name and designation,' Dar said. He and the Dance Master stared at each other hopelessly.

'I blame myself,' the Master said, drifting away, pounding one palm with his other fist. 'I should have refused the performance – told them we were under strength.'

'What about "Spheres and Fountains"?' someone asked.

The Master's face contorted. He reached out and touched the doorway, turning the big silvery disk transparent. 'Look for yourself. They're using a recording.'

A chorus of groans went up. Through the doorway, Naismith could see a line of Entertainers, apparently solid and real, gliding through the air.

There were tears in the Master's eyes. He reached out angrily, opaqued the doorway again. 'It couldn't be helped.

It couldn't be helped,' he said as he turned away.

After a moment the doorway cleared and a robot glided through. It was dark blue, a complex mathematical shape. It revolved slowly, picked out Dar, blinked its light at him. 'Come with me, please.'

Dar followed it to the doorway. The other Entertainers did not look at him.

The room beyond was tinted a dim violet rose, and Dar's heartbeat quickened. This was one of the Lenlu Din retreats, rooms whose location was known to no one but the owners and the robots.

Floating in the middle of the chamber was a hawk-nosed man in flaring striped garments. Various small memocubes and other equipment were scattered in the air around him. Faint music came from the wall.

'As you commanded, sir,' the robot said. It dipped, turned, and floated through the doorway again.

'Dar-Yani,' said the hawk-nosed man, consulting a memocube which he held in plump, jeweled fingers. 'Number 108, class 3.'

'Yes, sir.'

'You spoiled the formation of your dance troupe and caused acute esthetic pain to the Highborn,' said Hawknose severely.

'Yes, sir.'

'What punishment do you think you merit?'

Dar swallowed hard. 'Destruction, sir.'

'True. Well said. Now suppose I were to offer you a dangerous task instead – something to make up for your fault?'

'Sir, you would be most lenient.'

'So I think, myself. Well, Dar-Yani—' Hawknose consulted another memocube, pressing its sides impatiently until he had the information he wanted. 'You know, I suppose, that we have word from the future that a Zug has somehow got through the Barrier.'

'Yes, sir.'

'It will be necessary to kill it. The Shefthi, as you also know, are no longer with us.'

Dar's throat was dry. 'Yes, sir.'

'We are trying to retrieve one Shefth in order to kill this Zug, but in case of failure, it will be necessary for someone else to do it. Do you follow me?'

'Sir, I am untrained – I have fought Lenlu Om, but a Zug—'

'Quite understood. You need not be afraid of failure. At this time, we merely want to ascertain if an Entertainer *can* kill a Zug. We are not counting too much on you, Dar-Yani; however, do your best, do your best.' He smothered a yawn. 'You will have one hour with the training machines in which to perfect your approach. Then a robot will take you to the doorway into the Old City. As you know, there are Zugs in plenty there. The crucial thing to remember—'

5

The voice receded, became unintelligible. Naismith awoke.

The dream had been so vivid that for a moment it seemed absurd to find himself in darkness, pressed by gravity into a spring mattress, with the smells of fabric and dust around him.

He sat up in the darkness, realizing that another night had passed without his coming any closer to a solution. The simplest thing would be to give in to the aliens—

'No!' he said aloud, swinging his legs out of bed. He showered, shaved, prepared food and ate it.

After breakfast, he sat with paper and pencil, drawing up another list:

1. Capitulate.
2. Escape and hide.
3. Resist passively.

He drew lines through the first two entries; the first was out of the question, the second impossible. The third seemed to offer some hope; but he sensed in his bones that it would never succeed. Again he thought of a chessboard. A player under attack, his king driven by a series of checks toward the mating square, had only one chance: not to be driven passively, but to attack in turn.

He crumpled the paper, tossed it aside, stood up. Slowly a plan began to take shape in his mind.

In the first place, he must assume that he was under constant observation, even here in his own apartment. Even if he had the money, he could not take the risk of buying a weapon of any kind.

He looked at his broad, powerful hands, the thick fingers. Once, challenged by another student, he had bent a piece of iron pipe in half. The aliens had already made it clear that they were afraid of him ... and, Naismith told himself grimly, they had good reason.

He set about acting a part for an invisible audience. Preparing to go out, he counted the change in his pockets, closed his fist on the few coins with a gesture of anger.

He walked for an hour through the streets of Beverly Hills, head down, shoulders slumped; then he visited an ex-classmate and tried to borrow money. The man was an electrical engineer named Stevens; he looked startled at Naismith's request, but handed over five dollars, apologizing, 'Sorry I'm a little short this week, Naismith, but if this is any help—'

Naismith took it, walked two blocks as before, then abruptly threw the money into the gutter. He said aloud, 'I've got to give in to them. I'm licked.' He took a deep breath, turned back and picked up the crumpled bill he had just thrown away. He smoothed it out, his face set in lines of despair and resignation. When a cab cruised by, he hailed it and gave the aliens' address. Outside, he was all surrender; inside, all murder.

He knocked at the red door. A voice called, 'Come in – the door is not locked.'

The room was as Naismith had seen it before. Churan sat behind his table, staring across at him with hooded amber eyes. The Lall creature was leaning against a bookcase to his right, arms folded, smoking a cigarette. Neither spoke.

Naismith moved forward. 'I've come to tell you to call off your dogs.'

Churan's smile widened slightly; Lall glanced at him and blew a long plume of smoke from her lips.

Naismith measured the distance to the two aliens. Half a step nearer—

'Tell me your plans,' he began, then launched himself into motion. One hand stabbed out for Churan's throat, the other reached for Lall's. Both missed their targets; his hands closed on air.

Yet the aliens had not moved. With a chill of horror, Naismith realized that his arms had passed completely through their bodies.

Churan, his face abominably close, began to laugh. After a moment Lall joined in.

Naismith stumbled backward. The two aliens glanced at each other, their eyes welling tears of merriment.

'A nice try, Professor Naismith,' said Lall. 'But not good enough.'

Then, in an instant, both the aliens were gone. Shaking, incredulous, Naismith nerved himself to step forward again and stare at the place where they had been.

On the floor, between Churan's chair and the bookcase, lay a small black machine with dull red lights fading in its lenses. When he leaned down to touch it, a numbing electric shock made him jerk his hand back.

The room was empty. But as he backed away, the aliens' laughter swelled out again from nowhere, malicious and mocking. Then, close behind him, Lall's voice whispered in his ear, 'A reminder, Professor—'

As he tried to turn, something struck the side of his head. The room darkened.

Without transition, he was in the City, floating in the center of a vast chamber of carved and fretted ivory, empty and shadowed. When he moved, the faint sibilance of his garments echoed back in sinister whisperings from the walls: 'Shhh ... shhh ...'

He knew that he was going to die. He had made his farewells to all his friends and the members of his troupe; had returned his possessions to the central store; and had himself expunged his name from the register of Entertainers. In a real sense, he was already dead: Dar-Yani no longer existed. He was only a nameless and faceless body, a remnant, a fiction, drifting through the memories of the Old City.

It was the first time he had been here since the building of the New City. It was strange to see these once familiar rooms and corridors in their desolation. Built of material substances, painstakingly decorated and ornamented over a thousand years, this had been the real and only City until the growing Zug threat had forced mankind to leave it for new chambers of Zug-proof energy. After the Barrier was put up, it was said, the people would all move back here; but the man who had been Dar-Yani would not live to see it.

An injustice? Perhaps. He thought of the greenskins, and his lips curled. It was all well enough for them to revolt when they felt their case was desperate. But the Entertainers had their traditions.

He paused to listen. The unfamiliar armor was tight around his chest, and his palms were sweaty where they gripped the stock of the gun.

The only sounds were the ceaseless, unnerving whisperings that echoed back from the walls. He hesitated, then moved toward one of the hundred corridors that gave exit from the room.

Here, in this famous concourse, Ito-Yani had given his recitals, holding an audience of thousands spellbound for hours. Now, like the rest of the Old City, it had been abandoned to those chill monsters which ...

He froze, listening with all his body. Down the dimness of the corridor, there had been a faint sound.

When the beast attacks, the training machine had told

him, *you will have at most two seconds to aim and fire. Should you survive the first blow ...*

Another sound, nearer.

He backed away from the opening, with a panicky sense that he was not ready, it was too soon, he needed more time...

The noise came again; now he saw a pale glimmer of motion down in the depths.

Every cell of his body shrieked its terror; but he stayed where he was, teeth bared, his hand tight on the gun.

Without warning, the distant shape grew near. It floated toward him silently, with incredible speed. Through the view disk of his helmet he could see its tiny red eyes, its claws outstretched. As if in a nightmare, he strove to bring up the heavy gun, but he could not move fast enough. As the monster loomed nearer, its fanged jaws opened and—

Naismith sat up on the floor, with the hoarse echo of his own shout echoing in his ears. His head hurt. He was shaking all over, covered with cold sweat. In the darkness, the monster was still looming nearer, still opening its jaws ...

The smell of his own fear was thick in his nostrils. His hands found the shape of an overturned chair ... *Where was he?*

He got to his feet, fumbled in his pockets for a match. The flame showed him a littered carpet, books and papers stacked against the walls...

He remembered his last moment of consciousness, and his fingers went to the swelling over one ear.

The match went out. Naismith lit another, found the lamp and turned it on. The machine he had seen on the carpet was no longer there. The apartment was empty.

Naismith sat down for a moment with his head in his hands. Then, with sudden decision, he rose and went to the visiphone in the corner. He punched a number.

The screen lighted; Dr. Wells' brown, seamed face looked up pleasantly. 'Oh, hello, Naismith. How have you been getting along? Is anything the matter?'

'Wells,' said Naismith tensely, 'you told me once there

was a crash method we could employ to break my amnesia, if everything else failed.'

'Well, yes, but we're not down to that yet, man. Be patient, give the routine methods a chance to work. Now, your next appointment—' He reached for his calendar.

'I can't wait,' Naismith told him levelly. 'How dangerous is this method, and what does it involve?'

Wells put his muscular hands together under his chin. 'It's dangerous enough. Some people have been driven into psychosis by it – it's nothing to fool with, I assure you. Essentially, what it amounts to is a psychic leverage to bring up the material the patient's mind is holding back. Sometimes, when it does come up, it shocks him so that he goes off into a psychotic state. There are good reasons for loss of memory sometimes, Naismith.'

'I'll take the chance,' Naismith said. 'When are you free?'

'Well now, hold on a minute – I haven't said *I'd* take the chance. Really, Naismith, my advice to you is to wait—'

'If you won't do it, I'll find another psychiatrist who will.'

Wells looked unhappy. 'In this town, that wouldn't be impossible. Come over, Naismith, and we'll discuss it anyhow.'

Wells finished arranging the head clamps and stepped back, glancing at the meters on the control unit beside the couch. 'All right?' he asked.

'Get on with it.'

Wells' brown fingers hesitated on the knob. 'You're sure it's what you want?'

'I told you my reasons,' Naismith said impatiently. 'Come on, let's get started.'

Wells turned the knob; the machine clicked on, and a low hum was audible. Naismith felt a curious tickling sensation in his skull, and resisted an impulse to reach up and tear off the head clamps.

'In previous sessions,' Wells said, 'we've taken you back through your hospital days, covered that fairly well, and your college experiences after you got out. Now let's see if we can bring up a little sharper detail from one of those memories.' He turned a dial; the tickling sensation grew stronger.

'I direct your attention to your first day in the Air Force Medical Center,' said Wells. 'Try to recapture the image of your first waking recollection. The first thing you remember, on waking up....'

Naismith tried to concentrate. He had a vague recollection of whiteness – white sheets, white uniforms....

Watching him, Wells did something at the control unit. Instantly a vivid scene leaped up in Naismith's mind, so clear and detailed that it was almost like living it over again.

'Yes?' said Wells alertly. 'Describe what you see and hear.'

Naismith clenched his fists involuntarily, then tried to relax. 'Young doctor just came into my room. I can see his face as clearly as yours. About thirty, heavy cheeks, cheerful-looking, but his eyes are shrewd. Looked at my chart, then at me. "How are we feeling today?" Nurse glanced at me and smiled, then went out. Big, pleasant room – green walls, white curtains. I said, "Where am I?"' Naismith paused, frowning in surprise. 'I didn't remember anything ... not anything. Not even the language – he –' Naismith twisted suddenly on the couch.

'Easy,' said Wells. 'Can you tell me his reply?'

Naismith clenched his jaw. 'I can *now*. He said, "What language is that, old fellow?" But I didn't understand it!' Naismith rose to one elbow. 'He was talking English, and I didn't understand a word!'

Wells pressed him back, looking worried. 'Easy,' he repeated. 'We knew you were totally amnesic after the crash. You had to relearn everything. Don't let the vividness of this recollection—'

'*But what language was* I *speaking?*' Naismith demanded ferociously. 'When I asked him. "Where am I?"'

Wells looked startled. 'Can you repeat the actual sounds?'

'*Glenu ash i?*' said Naismith after a moment, with closed eyes. Tension was mounting in him; he could not lie still.

His jaw muscles were painfully tight, and he could feel his forehead beginning to sweat. 'Do you recognize it?'

'I'm no linguist. It isn't German, or French or Spanish, I'm quite sure. But perhaps Rumanian, or Croatian, something from that general area? Is there any influence of that kind in your background?'

'Not according to the records,' Naismith said tensely. Sweat was streaming down his face; his fists clenched and opened, clenched again. 'My parents were both native-born and lived in the Midwest all their lives. Both died in the Omaha dusting, and so did all my other relatives; I was the last one. And I nearly bought it.'

'Let's pass on,' said Wells. 'After this is over, I'll play that phrase back to Hupka or Leary, and see what they say. Let's try a little farther back now. Try to compose yourself.'

'All right.' Naismith straightened out on the couch, arms at his sides.

'I direct your attention now,' said Wells carefully, in a strained voice, 'to your last memory *before* waking up in the hospital. The last thing you remember.' He touched the controls again.

Naismith started, as another of those vivid images exploded in his mind. A landscape this time, misty and gray.

'The crash,' he said hoarsely, and licked his lips. 'Wreckage all the hell over – smoking.... Bodies—'

'Where are you?' Wells asked, bending nearer.

'About twenty yards from the fuselage,' Naismith said, with an effort. 'Buck naked, bleeding. ... It's cold. Bare ground. There's a body, and I'm bending over to see who it is. No face, all smashed. Dog tags. ... Good Christ!' He sat up abruptly, trembling.

Wells went pale under his tan and switched off the machine. 'What was it?'

'I don't know,' Naismith said slowly, fumbling in his mind for the image that was no longer there. 'I was reaching for the guy's dog tags, and then – I don't know what. A hell of a shock. Now it's gone.'

'We'd better call this a session,' said Wells, about to disconnect the control unit. 'Next time—'

'No!' Naismith seized his arm. 'We're close to it now, I can feel it. I'm not going to quit. Turn that thing on.'

'I don't think it's wise, Naismith,' said Wells soothingly. 'You're reacting too strongly; this is powerful stuff, don't forget.'

'One more try,' said Naismith. 'I can take one more, then we'll pass it till next time.' He held Wells' eyes with his.

'All right, then,' said Wells reluctantly. 'Let's see. ...'

Naismith lay back. The hum and the tickling in his skull began again. 'I direct your attention,' said Wells, 'to your childhood. Any scene from your childhood. Anything that comes to mind.'

Naismith went rigid. Something swam up toward his conscousness, something so dreadful that if he saw it, he would go mad. Then it was gone.

So it had been a flop. Angrily, as he stood on the path outside Wells' home, Naismith massaged his temples with his fingers. All he had got out of the whole thing was a headache.

He stood in angry indecision for a moment. One by one, his possibilities of action were being cut off. Ever since that first day, in class—

A thought that had been hovering at the back of his mind began to take definite shape. It was true that everything had started there, while he was under the influence of the Hivert Duplicator. ... Was it possible that his experiences since then – the dreams, everything – were due to some alien tampering with that mechanism? Had they planted something in it to exercise a subtle compulsion on his mind?

Once he had asked himself the question, he could not let it alone. He started off down the path toward the tube entrance.

The headache got no better and no worse. It felt as though the clamps Wells had put on his head were still there, and although it was senseless, he could not get rid of the impulse to brush them away.

Going to Wells had been a mistake. All the discomfort, the paraphernalia, the time wasted, and still they had got absolutely nothing from the blank period that ended four years ago. Some few bits of memory from his time in the hospital after the crash – more than they had got previously – then nothing at all.

He got off at the University stop, walked to the Science Building in bright sunlight. A few students he passed stopped and looked after him; but he met no one he knew well, and no one spoke to him.

As he climbed the rear stair to the classrooms, he met jittery Donald Klemperer coming down, followed by a young preparator named Irving; both were wearing lab smocks, and looked startled to see him. Klemperer was the youngest member of the Physics Department, an anxious, blinking youngster. Irving was dark, heavy and placid.

'Oh, uh, Professor Naismith,' Klemperer stammered. 'Professor Orvile said—'

'Have you been taking over my classes?' Naismith asked pleasantly, continuing to climb the stairs past them.

'Yes, yes I am, but what I wanted to say—'

'How did the demonstration go today?' Naismith was at the head of the stairs, turning his head to look back. Klemperer and Irving, craning up, both had their mouths open.

'All right, ah pretty well, but—'

'That's good, keep it up.' Naismith started briskly down the hall.

'But Professor Orvile said if I saw you, I was to be sure and get your *key*!' Klemperer wailed.

Naismith did not answer. He unlocked the door of the duplicator room, slipped inside, slammed it behind him. Reacting to his presence, the lights slowly glowed on.

He looked around the room, examining the familiar equipment as if he had never seen it before. The duplicator mechanism, in three metal cases grouped against one wall, and in the two units above and below the object platform, was a standard nine-gang Hivert Duplicator outfit. It had an object field six feet in radius, here marked off by a low railing. The table and apparatus were set up much as he had left them: the tank, the tau accumulator, the release mechanism, now pushed to one side. Several items had been added: a photometer and interferometer, a small theodolite, some prisms, the usual equipment for demonstrating the optical properties of quasi-matter. In addition, the heavy base-plate of a hydraulic jack had been bolted to the floor, and a small traveling crane had been positioned to take the weight of the tank when the table was removed.

Naismith recognized the preparations for the third in the series of quasi-matter demonstrations: Klemperer and Irving must have been setting them up just before he arrived.

He glanced thoughtfully at the tank itself. The liquid inside, still in the quasi-matter state, reflected light like a tankful of mercury. The reflections of the walls, the door and the equipment around the room were distorted by the tank's curvature, and by something else. From where he stood, Naismith could clearly see the image of the duplicator machinery on the wall to his left, whereas his own reflection was a barely visible stripe at the right rim of the tank.

With some difficulty, he got the front panels off all three units of the control mechanism, and examined the massed tubes and wiring inside. He was not an expert on the Hivert, but was generally familiar with its design, and as far as he could tell, there were no signs of anything unusual. The units in floor and ceiling were less readily accessible, but both were thick with dust and grime; obviously they had not been opened for months.

His ears caught a faint click, and he turned in time to see the door swing open.

In the doorway stood two broad men in maroon jackets. Light glinted from the guns in their hands. 'Hold it!' said one sharply.

Caught off balance, with no time to think, Naismith instinctively slammed one hand down onto the light button on the control pedestal. He pivoted in the same motion and kept going, while the room lights winked out and the room darkened, except for the broken shaft of illumination from the doorway.

Someone shouted. Naismith was moving fast, swinging around the corner of the table. There was a deafening roar as one of the guns went off; then Naismith was crouching, sheltered by the tank. Only two or three seconds had gone by.

In the ringing silence, one of the men called thinly, 'Come out of there, Naismith! You can't make it – there's only one door!'

By the flickering of the light from the doorway, Naismith could tell that both men had come farther into the room, moving apart, one to each side. Poised and alert, his head thudding steadily, Naismith was able to think with cold precision: *The tank rotates momentum 90° counterclockwise.*

Both hands went quickly to the tabletop. One closed on the heavy brass theodolite, the other snatched up two of the prisms.

In his mind he was keeping track of the two men's positions, diagramming them like an elementary problem in trigonometry. He waited until the last instant, then sprang up and threw the prisms at the man on his right.

The room roared again, with a volume of sound that made the walls shiver and hurt his eardrums. The glass tank dissolved into a hundred fragments. but the silvery cylinder of quasi-matter stood unchanged. As he ducked down behind the tank, Naismith heard the shots continue: three, four....

There was a faint clatter and a thump from the other side of the room, to his left.

Naismith risked a look: the man on his left was kneeling, arms crossed tightly over his stomach, head forward. His gun was on the floor. The man swayed and began to topple.

Naismith gathered himself, swung the heavy theodolite over the table with all his force, and instantly followed it, vaulting the table. The second man was down, off balance, having ducked to avoid the missile. He snapped one shot at Naismith, filling the room with sound: then Naismith was on top of him. Naismith felt a brief shock in one hand, and the man was sprawling limply under him, his neck unnaturally bent.

Naismith was up again almost without a pause, running out the door, past the white faces of Klemperer and Orvile; then down the stairs, out into the sunshine. He discovered that he was bleeding freely from a cut on one cheek, probably where one of the slivers of glass had struck him.

Realizing abruptly how fast he had been moving, he forced himself to walk at a normal pace across the lawns toward the tube entrance. A few students were gathered around a gray and blue copter parked on the lawn: the bubble was empty, the blades still. On impulse, Naismith went that way. A prickle of uneasiness went up his spine as he walked. It had been too quick: he had not had time to do more than act instinctively. There had been a threat to his life; he had met it with the means at hand, making one of his attackers shoot the other, by deflection from the kinetically inert quasi-matter. If he had thought at all, he had assumed the two men were gunsters hired by Lall and Churan. But...

He was at the copter, ignoring the students who turned to stare. Inside the bubble, a radio voice was muttering indistinguishably. Naismith opened the door, stepped up and leaned his head in to listen.

The uniformed patrolman in the tiny visiscreen was saying: '... detention and interrogation. This man is wanted for the murder of Dr. Claude R. Wells, a psychiatrist at the University of California in Los Angeles. Wells was battered to death, and his office completely wrecked an hour ago. Naismith is considered extremely dangerous. He is not known to be armed, but is to be approached with caution. His description again, W.M.A., six feet two inches ...'

The last words barely registered. Naismith turned away, with a roaring of doom in his head. When they saw his face, the students looked alarmed and backed off. He went through them, past them, moving like a somnambulist.

He could not even reject what he had heard in disbelief.

He had realized instantly at the first words from the copter radio, that he had no memory of Wells at all beyond that frightening unseen thing that had come up out of his childhood. After that, a blank.

'Struggle against us,' the Lall creature had said. And he had done it; and this was the crushing result. He had killed Wells and two detectives. Now he was 'ready'; he had nowhere left to go, except to Lall and Churan.

Behind him a weak, distant voice was calling: 'Hey ...' came faintly over the lawns. 'Hey, stop him! Stop him! Hey ...'

Naismith glanced back, saw two doll-figures emerging from the Science Building. One had white hair, and he identified it instantly as Orvile. Both were running, waving their arms.

The students around Naismith turned their heads indecisively from the two figures to Naismith. Like most people, they were slow to react. Naismith turned his back on them, careful not to move too quickly, and started to walk away.

At the last moment, a husky senior blocked his path. As he opened his mouth to speak, Naismith straight-armed him and began to run. His last glimpse of the senior showed him on one leg, windmilling his arms for balance, his mouth all amazement.

Naismith sprinted. He had taken four strides when the sound he dreaded broke out behind him: a chorus of yells from many young throats; the sound of a mob in pursuit.

As he ran at full speed toward the tube entrance, a second police copter was sidling down out of the sky.

6

With the sound of the mob in his ears, Naismith ducked into the tube entrance and went down the stairs three at a time. He had one chance in a thousand. If there should be a train just pulling out—

The station was empty.

He saw that in one instant. In the next, at the edge of his vision, he saw a door open. He whirled. It was the door to a maintenance room; as it swung open, he saw it was blank except for ventilation louvers, and a number painted in white.

Inside the room, dark in a shimmer of faint colors, stood Miss Lall with Churan behind her. She held out her hand. 'Come in!'

He sprang toward the doorway, aware as he did so that there was something abnormal about the walls of the room. They were curved and insubstantial, with a soap-bubble shimmer about them; they were partly transparent. Beyond them, he could dimly make out the real walls of the room, with clothing hanging on hooks, a mop leaning against one corner.

Then he was inside. Lall sidled past him and closed the door. Churan remained seated. The three of them looked at each other. They were enclosed and huddled together by an oval shell of transparent, streaming color. The light was strange; it was like being inside an egg made of rushing shadows.

Outside, an instant later, the rattle of footsteps and a frantic baying of voices poured down the stairs, onto the platform.

Naismith took a deep breath, let it go, relaxed deliberately with his hands at his sides. 'All according to plan?' he asked ironically.

'According to plan, Mr. Naismith,' said Churan. He was seated on a stool which appeared to be part of the substance of the shadow-egg. The dancing prismatic colors streamed out from the base of this stool and disappeared at the apex of the shell over their heads.

Churan's stubby, short-fingered hands lay casually upon the blue-steel object in his lap. With a shock, Naismith recognized the machine that had disappeared from the closet of his Beverly Hills apartment.

Churan's eyes flickered. 'We have saved your life, Mr. Naismith,' he said hoarsely.

'All right, let's say you did. You must have done it for some reason. Here I am. Just what is it that you want?'

Lall, her eyes shining, said something swift and emphatic in a language that sounded tantalizingly familiar to Naismith – a curious combination of liquids and deep gutturals. Churan nodded, wet his lips nervously. 'We want you to come with us,' he said. 'A long journey, Mr. Naismith – twenty thousand years. Does that interest you?'

'What if I say no?'

Churan's amber eyes glinted briefly. 'We want you to come willingly, Mr. Naismith.'

Naismith gave a mirthless bark of laughter. 'Is that why you did all this – killed Ramsdell and Mrs. Becker?'

The woman bent toward him slightly. 'I'm not sure you understand, Mr. Naismith. The machine killed Mr. Ramsdell and Mrs. Becker. It is tuned to our mind pattern – yours, his and mine. You see, for anyone else, it is not safe to touch. A precaution against theft.'

Naismith felt his anger growing in spite of himself. 'Are you saying that two people died just for nothing – just because you wanted to get that machine into my hands?'

'No, on the contrary,' said Churan. 'Sending the machine to you was merely a device to kill Mr. Ramsdell, so that you would be suspected of murder. Our aim was to weaken your associations here. You were too well convinced that you were really Gordon Naismith.'

Outside, the noise of the crowd was dwindling; Naismith could hear isolated querulous voices calling from one end of the platform to the other. From time to time, someone would approach the maintenance room, try the knob, find it locked, and go away again.

Defeated, he made his decision. 'All right, I'm ready. Let's go.'

Lall and Churan exchanged a quick glance. Then the man's stubby fingers moved on the surface of the machine.

Naismith watched in fascination as the inlays, which had resisted all his efforts, depressed and moved under Churan's fingertips. As they did so, although there was no sense of motion, the walls of the maintenance room, hanging garments, mops and all, gently receded. In the act of turning, Naismith felt a psychic shock as the closed, shadowy door drifted through his own body.

Then they were moving across the station, a foot or two higher than the young men who stood in postures of arrested motion, scattered here and there about the platform. There was no sound. Every form was still, although some were caught in mid-stride. Faces were contorted, eyes glared blindly.

Moving at the same ever pace, they drifted into the wall of the station. Another moment of darkness, then they emerged, on a shallow upward slant, into the open air.

Naismith watched everything with intense concentration, trying to fathom the relationship between their movements and Churan's handling of the machine.

'What I fail to understand,' he said abruptly, 'is how the energies you are using can be contained in so small a space.'

'They are not, Mr. Naismith,' said Lall with a look of respect. 'The forces we use are generated in the future. This machine that you see is only the control unit. We call it—' She uttered two throaty monosyllables. 'In English, what would it be?' She paused, and said doubtfully, 'Time sphere? No, because it is not a sphere. But the name means something that is lowered in time, as you lower a bathysphere in the ocean. How would you say – you ought to know this, Mr. Naismith – a temporo- . . . ?'

Outside, the bright campus was like a color transparency: the two copters, the students on the lawn, all were caught in one frozen moment. Naismith stared in fascination as the shadow-egg drifted, now more rapidly, eastward across the lawns. Buildings, flame trees and people receded in perspective – not like a photograph now, but like some incredibly detailed and lifelike miniature model.

'Temporoscaphe?' he suggested wryly, after a moment.

'Good, temporoscaphe. But it is a very ugly word. . . . You see, we can control our position in both space and time. Just now, we move in space while remaining fixed in time. Later on, the other way around.'

Below, the landscape was now flowing back more rapidly. Sunlight glinted yellow off the tip of some building on the northern horizon. Rising on a long slant, they were now passing over Burwash Park. Naismith could see the gravel walks, the pedestrians frozen in place like bright-colored dolls, the silvery lake and the handball courts. It flowed away and was gone; the densely packed buildings of metropolitan Los Angeles swam into view, all in the same unearthly silence.

Standing there in the confined space of the shadow-egg, Naismith was abruptly aware of something that had been at the edge of his consciousness: the smell. It was cheap perfume, with an undertone, almost masked, that he recognized: the same cold, musky odor that he had smelled in Churan's office. Looking at the two of them now with renewed attention, he realized again how quite astoundingly ugly they were when seen together. What might have been an accidental cast of features in Lall – the flat, wide-nostriled nose, the long amber eyes, the thin mouth – became, in this doubled image, the pure stuff of ugliness. They were like two painted frogs, there in the shadow-egg, both staring at him with unwinking amber eyes – frogs, obscenely vivisected to stand erect and wear human clothing. And remembering the cold touch of Lall, Naismith shivered.

The foothills were sliding away beneath them now, yellow-brown and bare in the sunlight, then the mountains rose slowly into view. Naismith glimpsed sunlight winking from the windows of a canyon-perched house, tiny with distance. As they crossed the mountains, still gaining altitude, he could see the whole circle of the horizon, misty blue, with flecks of cirrus floating high in the pale vault. Something else caught his eye, a bright glint above the clouds, rapidly coming nearer. Now he could almost make it out; now it grew plain – a blue and silver Trans Am airliner. They were going to pass it almost on the same level. As it swelled nearer, brilliant and solid in the sunlight, Naismith flinched involuntarily; he could see every rivet in its polished skin. He could see, too, that it was hanging absolutely motionless in the air, as if embedded in gelatin. Behind the windshield, the pilot and copilot were stiff wax dummies; faint spears of flame were frozen in the jets. It whipped past and dwindled behind them, still hanging immovable.

The two aliens were watching him with intent, unreadable expressions. Naismith's lips were dry. He said, more harshly then he had intended, 'Where are we going?'

'Not so far now, Mr. Naismith,' said Churan. Below, the round world was rolling back at an incredible speed; there was a glint of silver that Naismith recognized as Boulder Dam; then the mighty scar of the Grand Canyon, filled with shadow, passed beneath. Then there were more mountains, and a threadlike river that must be the Colorado. Down on the plain beyond the mountains, Naismith caught sight of a city sprawled like a scattering of silver dominoes. It glittered in the parched land. 'Denver,' he said.

'Not the city itself,' said Churan, glancing down at the machine in his lap. 'We use it for a landmark.' Now his pudgy brown fingers were dancing over the machine, and Naismith saw the odd-shaped inlays depress one after another, glimpsed a shimmer of light that floated briefly over the machine. Then there was a spot of angry red light that pulsed slowly and regularly; then more rapidly as they crossed the city, slowly now, then more rapidly still as the shadow-egg drifted to a stop; and after a moment the red light shone steadily, with the faintest suggestion of a shimmering motion. The shadow-egg came to rest.

'From Los Angeles to Denver,' said Naismith, 'in – what? Five minutes? Four?'

'In one sense, no time at all,' said Lall. 'You realize this is still the same instant as when we left the tube station. No time has elapsed.'

Churan grinned up at him, showing yellow stubs of teeth. 'Now we have reached the right position in space,' he said. 'Therefore we shall begin to move in time. Are you ready, Mr. Naismith?'

Without waiting for an answer, he touched the machine again, and as if in response, the whole vast landscape beneath them dimmed, went dark, glowed to light again. Looking up, Naismith was in time to see the sun arching overhead like a fireball. It plunged into the western horizon with a flicker of red; then all was dark again. Light! The sun sprang up in the east, hurled itself overhead, plunged, and the world was dark. Light! Dark! Light! In the shadow-egg, Naismith saw the faces of Lall and Churan lit by the flickering alternation of days and nights. The landscape below, trembling in the swift waves of darkness and light, was tortured, changing, shaking itself into new forms. Naismith saw the city put out new tentacles, undergo writhing transformations, sprout taller buildings. It was like a grotesque animated film: the city had a rhythm of growth, rest, growth again.

Then, abruptly, there was a gigantic crater where the eastern half of the city had been. The growth cycle stopped. Naismith, rigid with fascination, saw areas of the city darken slowly, saw parts of it collapse into black ruin. 'What year?' he asked hoarsely.

'Toward the end of the nineties, I think,' said Lall's indifferent voice. 'It's not important.'

'Not important!' said Naismith automatically, but his voice died away as he watched the landscape below. The dead metropolis sank. It went down as if into quicksand; the earth visibly swallowed it. Then there was only a featureless plain, shimmering in the ghostly twilight. For what seemed like hours, there was no change.

Again Churan touched the machine. The flickering alternation of days and nights abruptly stopped. It was early evening, the clear sky darkening to a steely blue in which one or two stars were visible. The whole landscape, as Naismith looked around from his elevated position, was unearthly vacant and still. Not a roof, or a wall, or the trace of a road in the whole immense plain; not a light anywhere.

'What year?' he asked again.

No one answered. Churan touched the machine again and the shadow-egg began to drift down a long slant. They were skimming along at ground level now, through the knee-high grasses, toward a long, low mound that was just visible against the sky. The rest of the landscape was empty and dark.

As they drifted nearer, Naismith felt his body trembling with the shock of the visceral realization: this was real – this earth and its wet grass, this dark sky overhead. He was here, physically and inescapably.

Back in Los Angeles, Klemperer was taking his classes; someone else would be living in his Beverly Hills apartment ... No: they were all dead, dead and forgotten. The thought gave Naismith an extraordinary feeling of release and pleasure. Whatever was going to happen to him now, at least it would not be the safe, dull middle age he had looked forward to....

The mound they were approaching was both larger and nearer than it had appeared at first: perhaps thirty feet high, it was immensely long and straight, like one of the long barrows of Wiltshire. There were faint, earthy and woody smells in the cold air; but the black hulk of the mound hung silent and still. It was covered with the grasses that grew on the plain; on the skyline, against the moonlit clouds, Naismith could make out an occasional small shrub or tree.

They drifted into the blackness of the mound, which closed like a stifling curtain about their heads: then, with shocking suddenness, they were dazzled by golden light.

7

The room in which the shadow-egg now floated was a gigantic hall, paved with some gleaming, hard substance that was at once like marble and like metal. The golden light surrounded them only in a circle a few yards wide; but in the darkness beyond, Naismith could make out the gleam of a pillar, a distant wall, the shapes of furniture. Here was the future: and it was a deserted marble hall, buried under a mound of earth.

'What is this place?' Naismith demanded.

'A ship. A buried ship.' The echoes of Churan's voice whispered away into emptiness.

Naismith thought, *A ship. What* kind *of a ship?*

Now, in their circle of golden light, they were drifting along a spattered trail of bright-red pigment that began a few yards from the door. It looked as if paint had been dripped from a can along the shining floor, and then as if something else that Naismith could not quite understand had happened to it; the red pigment was crazed, checked, almost like weathered paint, and it was powdering away visibly, in streaks, toward the neraby wall.

Naismith bent to examine it as closely as he could through the shadow-egg. The only thing it suggested to him was a wind, drifting sand away from a dune: as if there were an impalpable slow wind here, drifting molecules of the red pigment across the floor....

He followed the red streaks to the wall, where, by squinting, he could make out a hairline of bright red along the join between wall and floor, running out of sight in either direction.

Did the floor reject anything that did not belong there?

Were dust, dirt, and red pigment swept away automatically and disposed of?

He straightened. The wall itself was of the same metallic marble as the floor – marble, if such a thing were possible, with flecks and veins of gold diffused uniformly through it. A few feet farther on there was an elaborate metal frame on the wall, and Naismith's interest quickened: but the frame was empty.

They floated through an archway, into a chamber only less gigantic than the first. Divans and tables stood here and there, in little, widely separated groups. Rich, soft rugs covered the floor; the red trail had been dripped indiscriminately over them, but here, too, the pigment was drifting away in long, faint streaks.

Some of the furniture looked like parodies of the overstuffed sofas and armchairs of his own time – puffed, bulging things, looking inflated rather than upholstered, and apparently made all in one unit – no separate cushions, no legs underneath.

Other pieces were built on a different principle: these were suspended, like porch gliders, from metal frameworks which rose to cylinders at either end. Between these cylinders swung chairs and sofas which appeared neither stuffed nor inflated, but were as if poured from some taffy-like substance, in silky bright colors and with a curious, eye-deceiving mistiness of surface. They were like shapes of bright smoke poured out of the cylinders at either end; and Naismith had the fanciful thought that if one turned off the mechanism in those cylinders, the chair or sofa would dissolve into vapor.

The red trail led them down a corridor lined with more of the empty metal frames; then through another archway, up a stair and around a gallery, over an empty chamber still larger than anything Naismith had seen; up another stair, down a hall, through another doorway.

The room they now entered was a small lounge from which other doorways opened on all sides. Naismith's first impression was of a fully illuminated room, more cluttered and disorderly than anything he had seen until now. Then his attention came to a sharp, incredulous focus: across the room, he saw the shadow-egg plainly reflected in a mirror ... but his own image was not there.

He blinked and looked again. There was no mistake; only the reflections of Lall and Churan stared back at him ... there was something wrong about them, too, in the way they were dressed, or—

Then the vision faded, became transparent and was gone.

There was no mirror. He realized abruptly that the image had not been reversed; his mind had supplied the mirror, an effort to make an intelligible pattern out of what he saw. But what *had* he seen? ...

Beside him, Churan laughed – a hoarse, nervous bark. 'Don't worry, Mr. Naismith,' he said.

Naismith turned. Both aliens were glancing at him with malicious smiles, but their attention seemed elsewhere. Churan made a final adjustment on the polished surface of the machine as the shadow-egg touched the carpet: then, leaning upon the machine with one hand as if it were a tabletop, he got his legs out from under it and stood up. Over the stool on which he had been sitting, the machine hung in air, unsupported and immovable.

Churan exchanged a few words with Lall; both looked serious and intent. Bending over the machine, Churan did something to it that Naismith could not follow: and the shadow-egg burst like a soap bubble.

They were standing in the middle of the brilliantly lighted room, all three; Churan tucked the machine under his arm like a briefcase.

There was movement in one of the doorways, and a small creature walked out into view. Naismith had to look twice to see that it was a child.

Lall bent over the creature, smoothing its dull black hair mechanically with one hand. The child spoke to her in a high, thin whine; she answered perfunctorily and pushed it away. With an incurious glance at Naismith, the child stumped off on its thick legs, sat down and began to play with a rag doll.

It was a quite incredibly ugly creature, greenish-brown-skinned, with sullen features. It looked like a caricature of Lall or Churan, everything about it coarsened and exaggerated.

'Is this your child?' Naismith asked, turning to Lall.

She nodded. 'It is a female – her name is Yegga.' She added a sharp sentence to the child, which was picking its nose; it left off and screamed once at its mother, without changing its sullen expression, then bent over its doll once more.

Naismith glanced around the room. Clothing was strewn over chairs and carpet; there were crumpled papers, even bits of food dropped here and there.

The high walls were paneled in vivid magenta and ivory: the ivory, Naismith discovered, was the wall itself, a dull, textureless surface; the wide magenta strips were hangings of the same substance as the suspended furniture, and had the same smoky outlines. Some of the chairs were of the same bright magenta; others were electric blue or ivory; the deep-piled carpet was apple green. The clothes piled carelessly here and there were of all hues.

'You left her here when you went back to my time?' Naismith asked, indicating the child.

Lall nodded again. 'She would have interfered with our work.'

'What if something had happened, and you'd never come back?'

'But we knew we would come back, Mr. Naismith,' said Churan, stepping nearer. 'We saw ourselves arrive, just as we saw ourselves leave just now . . . remember?'

A tingling sensation went down Naismith's spine as, with a renewed shock, he thought of the vision he had seen. If Churan were telling the truth, for an instant, just then, time had been doubled back on itself.

Naismith sat down on one of the armchairs, watching Churan as he stepped to the wall, opened a panel, and thrust the machine inside. Lall was stretching herself, looking relieved but abstracted, like any housewife returning after an absence.

'Let me understand this,' Naismith said vehemently. 'You knew that your mission would be successful, then – because you saw yourselves coming back with me, before you left?'

'Yes, we knew.' Churan began unfastening his jacket and shirt, pulling them off. He threw them on the nearest sofa with a grunt of relief. His hairless chest from the neck down, and his arms as far as the elbow, were a brownish-green color, the green of algae; it was apparently the natural color of his skin.

'Sit down, Mr. Naismith,' said Lall, taking off her blouse. 'Dial for some food, Gunda.' Her body, the same brownish-green as Churan's, was squat and soft-looking; the proportions were not quite human. Their bodies were mamalian, but entirely hairless, and, compared with a human being of Naismith's time, hardly sexed at all. Lall's breasts were almost as small and flat as Churan's.

The child glanced up from its play, then bent over again. It was, Naismith saw with a shock of distaste, pushing long pins or wedges of metal into the soft body of the doll.

'There's a paradox here, then,' he said, looking away with an effort. 'Why not turn me over to your earlier selves? Then you wouldn't have had to go at all.'

'No paradox. If we did that, it would pinch out the loop; then we would have to go just the same.' Seeing Naismith's frown, Churan added, 'Think of it as a short circuit, Mr. Naismith; then you will understand.'

Ignoring the two men, Lall dropped her remaining garments and left the room. Churan, wearing nothing but sandals, went to one of the wall panels and paused with his hand on it. 'You would like some food?' he said to Naismith. 'Something hot?'

'I'm not hungry,' Naismith said.

'But you must eat to live. Let me offer you something, Mr. Naismith; perhaps you will like it.' Pulling the panel aside, he rapidly thumbed down several movable strips, checkered green and white, which seemed painted on the wall and yet slid freely under his thumb. Interested, Naismith moved nearer, but Churan finished aligning the strips, closed the panel, opened another one. He reached in, took out steaming dishes one after another, and dropped them casually on a low, round table. 'Please sit down, Mr. Naismith. I am going to wash now, then we shall eat and have a talk.' He smiled, showing his yellow stumps of teeth, and followed Lall into the adjoining room. The child got up and followed him, squalling something in its thin voice.

After a moment Naismith began to examine the food. There were four dishes, each containing a different mess, from which the diners were evidently intended to help themselves with their fingers. One was dark green and smelled like seaweed; one cream-colored, with pink lumps; one was a pasty mound; and the fourth was a varicolored mixture, with shreds of what looked like meat and vegetables in it.

From the other room came the muffled sound of voices. Naismith turned, stepped to the wall where he had seen Churan put the machine away.

He touched the panel, tried to move it aside as Churan had done, but the stuff was half like cloth and half like water – it resisted, then seemed almost to flow between his fingers. The look and feel of it, no more definite of outline than it had seemed from a distance, were subtly unpleasant, and after a moment he gave it up. As he turned, Lall came out of the adjoining room, fastening a short-sleeved white tunic around her waist. Her skin, where it was visible, was now a uniform brown-tinted green; she had removed her makeup. So had Churan, who appeared behind her, dressed in sleeveless red pajamas. His pointed beard was gone; the whole shape of his face seemed different, and uglier, without it. Now Naismith realized something that had eluded him before – the Churan in the other shadow-egg had been beardless.

The child wandered in, seized a bowl of food from the table, spilling it, and took it to a corner, where it sat down and began stuffing itself.

'It is good to be clean again,' said Lall. 'Pardon me, I did not think. Perhaps you would also like to bathe before eating, Mr. Naismith?'

'Later,' Nasmith said. 'Right now, I want to talk.'

Churan had seated himself at the table, and was tucking gobs of food into his mouth, using two fingers like a spoon. He grunted, chewing a mouthful that bulged his cheeks. 'Good.'

Lall sat down and offered Naismith the place beside her. 'Please help yourself, Mr. Naismith. Forks are not used here, but I am sure you can manage.'

'I'm not hungry,' Naismith said impatiently. He sat; the cushioned stool was uncomfortably low, and he had to jack-knife his legs to get them under the table. 'You eat, and I'll ask the questions. To begin with—'

'Something to drink, then. Gunda, a cup of water.'

Without looking up, Churan reached out to the wall beside him, opened the panel, and withdrew a porcelain cup which he set on the table.

Naismith took it in his hand; it was half filled with clear water; the cup was chill to the touch. He hesitated, then put it down. Bathing had apparently removed the aliens' perfume as well as their brown makeup; under the odors of the food and water, he could smell the cold, reptilian scent of their bodies. 'I'm not thirsty, thank you.'

Lall paused with her fingers in the dish of cream-colored substance. 'Mr. Naismith, our foods may be unfamiliar to you, but surely you can drink our water, which is chemically pure.'

Naismith stared at her. 'Even water can be poisoned, or drugged.'

'Drugged!' she repeated, and wiped her fingers slowly on the side of her patterned tunic. 'Mr. Naismith, if you could be drugged, do you think we would have been to so much trouble to get you here?' She paused, glanced at her fingers, then sucked them slowly clean. She pushed the dish away from her, leaned her elbow on the table, staring at him. The folds of her eyelids were odd, not quite human. 'Think about it, Mr. Naismith. Do you remember Bursar Ramsdell – and the lawyer, Jerome? The peculiar things they did and said? *They* were drugged; that was simple to do.' Churan had stopped eating to listen; his amber eyes were narrow and watchful. 'But you are an altogether different problem, Mr. Naismith. Don't you realize, haven't you any idea— Think a moment, have you ever been ill?'

'My memory goes back only about four years. I don't know.'

'But in those four years? An upset stomach? A cold? Even a headache?'

'I had a headache when you knocked me out, and another one when I left Wells' office this afternoon. I mean—' He groped for a word to express the time that had elapsed, gave it up.

'Indeed? I don't understand. Did he use drugs?'

'No, some gadget – a headband, with clamps.'

She raised her eyebrows. 'Ah, I see. And the gadget gave you a headache. But aside from that, can you remember any slightest illness?'

'No,' Naismith admitted.

'No, of course not. The Shefth does not become ill, cannot be drugged or hypnotized; his body rejects most poisons. He is *very* hard to deal with, Mr. Naismith; he must be treated with respect. So if you are thirsty, please drink without fear.'

Naismith glanced down at the cup of water, then at the two aliens who sat watching him, motionless and intent. 'I'll drink this,' he said slowly, 'when I understand one or two things a little better.'

'Ask,' said Lall, dipping up another lump of the cream-colored food.

'Let's begin with this place – you call it a ship. Who left it here, and why?'

'It's an interstellar liner. When the colonies were abandoned, in the hundred tenth century, there was no more need of it, they just left it. That was about a century ago.'

'Why did you bring me here?'

'To teach you, Mr. Naismith – certain things which—'

Naismith made an impatient gesture. 'I mean why *here*? Why couldn't you have taught me these things, whatever they are, back in Beverly Hills?'

She chewed, swallowed. 'Let us say, there was a need to be inconspicuous. This is a dead period, for hundreds of years on either side. No one knows about this abandoned liner except us, and no one would think of looking here.'

Naismith knotted a fist impatiently, stared at the taut skin over the knuckles. 'This is getting us nowhere,' he growled. 'You talk about a dead period, Shefthi, Zugs – it's all Greek to me. How do I know there's a word of truth in it anywhere?'

'You do not,' said Churan, leaning forward earnestly. 'You're right, it is futile for us to talk about these things. Talk goes around and around, endlessly.' He made a circular motion. 'But there is another way.'

He got up, crossed to the opposite wall, where he opened one of the panels. He reached in and took out a metal framework, with an oblong box dangling from a strap. 'This, Mr. Naismith.'

Its resemblance to the machine Wells had used was obvious at a glance. Naismith pushed his stool back. 'No,' he said.

Churan paused, disconcerted. 'But I haven't even told you about it yet.'

'It doesn't matter – I've tried one. Once was enough.'

'You *tried* one?' Lall repeated with a disbelieving smile. 'Where was this?'

'At Wells' office. I blanked out, evidently— But you know all about that – that's why the police were after me, back there at the campus.'

Both aliens looked alarmed. Lall turned and shot a question at Churan – rapid guttural syllables, in which Naismith caught the name 'Wells'. Churan answered explosively, then both turned and stared at Naismith.

'This may be tremendously important, Mr. Naismith. Please describe the machine he used, and the effect it had on you.'

Naismith did so, as best he could. As he spoke, both aliens visibly relaxed; after a few moments, Lall raised her hand to stop him. 'That's enough, Mr. Naismith. It's apparent that this was not exactly the same kind of machine.'

'I never said it was. But nobody is going to monkey with my mind again, with *any* kind of machine.'

'What are you afraid of, Mr. Naismith?' Churan asked softly.

Naismith said nothing for a moment. Then: 'You're the one who ought to be afraid. I *killed Wells* while that machine was operating.'

'Evidently because there is something in your past that you subconsciously did not wish to remember. That is not hard to understand. Let me put it this way, Mr. Naismith. This machine will not bring back any of your own memories. Instead, it will add certain memories which you never had before.'

'It's out of the question,' Naismith said flatly. 'Teach me the ordinary way, if it's so damned important. Start with the language. Give me books, records, whatever there is. I happen to be quick at languages. Even if I weren't, you've got plenty of time.'

Churan shook his head. 'Books and records could be falsified, Mr. Naismith.'

'So could that thing.'

'No, it could not,' Churan said hoarsely, blinking with anger. 'When you experience it, you will know. *That* is why no other method will serve. It's not just a question of time, Mr. Naismith. You must be convinced, beyond any possible doubt, that what we are going to tell you is true.'

They looked at each other in silence for a moment.

'Why?' Naismith asked bluntly.

The two aliens glanced at each other with resigned expressions. Churan sat down, holding the helmet and the control unit on his lap.

'Mr. Naismith,' Lall said after a pause, 'what if you knew that the ruling class of your own people had *deliberately* thrown you back in time, to the year 1980, believing you would be killed?'

'Why should they do that?'

Her fingers stretched into claws, then relaxed. 'Because they are selfish and cowardly. After they had made up their minds to create the Barrier, they felt the Shefthi would be more a danger than a—'

'Wait,' said Naismith with an impatient gesture. 'The Barrier . . . tell me about that.'

'In our own time, the ruling caste found a way to make a Time Barrier that would pass only the Lenlu Din into the future. It would be tuned to their mind patterns, you see; in that way, on the far side there would be no more Zugs, and also no more Lenlu Om. Just Lenlu Din, all by themselves, safe and contented. You understand? But it is not going to work. We know, because they are sending back messages through the Barrier. There is one Zug up there, still alive. And they are very frightened.' He grinned unpleasantly.

'If none of this has happened yet, what makes you so sure it's going to happen?'

The woman sighed. 'These are only ways of speaking. Surely you understand that by now, Mr. Naismith. From your point of view in 1980, all this "has not happened yet". But here were are. As for the Barrier, we know it exists in the future. We know it is going to work, except that one Zug will be left alive. As Gunda has just told you, we know all this because we have received messages from beyond the Barrier.'

Naismith sat back. 'The future can communicate with the past?' he asked disbelievingly.

'Haven't you seen that it can? Didn't we go back to the twentieth century, and scoop you up like a fish in a net?' Lall's amber eyes were brilliant, her fingers tense.

'Then why don't they simply tell their earlier selves to do things differently, and eliminate the trouble?'

'They can't find the trouble,' said Lall, her eyes shining. 'It is impossible for a Zug to pass through the Barrier alive. But their detectors show that there is one, and that's why they are so frantic. When we learned that, we saw our opportunity.' She leaned forward, intent, lips moist. 'We searched the main stem as far back as the twentieth century. Every anomaly above a certain value had to be investigated. It took *years*, subjective time. It was only the most incredible luck that we found you at all. Then we had to prepare this place; then go back to 1980 and learn the language, customs, everything, from the beginning. And now it all comes together. Because you see they are *desperate*. If you return, with some story of having built your own time generator, they will believe you – they have to, you are the last Shefth, and they need you.' Both aliens were breathing heavily, staring at Naismith across the low table.

'Then a Shefth can go through the Barrier?' asked Naismith.

'The Shefthi are Lenlu Din,' Churan answered. 'If they had let well enough alone, all the Shefthi would be on the other side of the Barrier, and there would be no problem with the Zug. But they didn't want any warriors in their safe future, without Zugs, without Lenlu Om. They would have killed you, but they were afraid. So they invented a story about an expedition to kill Zugs in the past, and threw you all back. At random, without destination. Without protection. The shock of landing was to kill you all. Even if it did not, without equipment you could never get back to bother them. That was their plan.'

'I see,' said Naismith.

'What is your reaction to this, Mr. Naismith?' Churan's voice was strained.

'If it's true, I'm ... very interested,' said Naismith. 'Now one more point. What's this about the Lenlu Om? You said the Barrier was to keep them out too. Who are they, or what are they?'

'We are Lenlu Om,' said Churan quietly. 'The name means "the Ugly People". We are their servants. They brought us from another place, centuries ago. We are not considered to be human.'

Naismith glanced up: the faces of all three aliens had turned hard and expressionless. He put the cylinder down carefully and stood up slowly, feeling their eyes on him.

'And all this,' he said, 'in more detail, you would have taught me with that thing.' He nodded toward the device in Churan's lap.

'As well as many other things. The language. We can teach you to speak it perfectly in less than two hours. And you must speak it perfectly. Then the City itself – the castes – forms of courtesy – a thousand and one things you must know, Mr. Naismith. You can learn it all by primitive methods, of course, but believe me, it is not worth the effort.'

'But you used so-called primitive methods to learn English.'

Churan hesitated. 'Yes and no. We employed the educator – we recorded disks from the thoughts of natives whom we captured and drugged. But that is not the same as having an edited subject disk all prepared. It was tedious, it took time. Then we also had to spend time establishing identities for ourselves. We took, I don't know, perhaps six months, subjective time. Without the educator, it would have taken years.'

Something that had been bothering Naismith came abruptly into focus, and he swung around, with one foot up on the bench, facing Churan. 'Tell me this,' he said. 'Why not simply go back, learn what you need to know – then put it all on one disk – *meet yourselves arriving*, and cut out all the trouble?'

Churan sighed. 'As I told you before, it would pinch out the loop. You cannot use time in that way.'

8

After a moment Lall and Churan yawned together like two frogs, showing the dark greenish roofs of their mouths: the effect was grotesquely unpleasant. 'We are tired,' Lall said. 'It is late.' She rose, followed by Churan, and led the way to the room opening off the far end of the lounge, opposite the one she and Churan had used. The child trailed after them, dragging its doll by one arm.

The door was closed, but opened at Lall's touch. She stood aside. 'This will be your sleeping room, Mr. Naismith. I think you will find all you need.'

The three stood waiting. Naismith glanced in; there was a low bed, footstool, some ambiguous, half-real draperies on the wall. He made no move to enter. 'Thank you,' he said.

'You will sleep here?' Lall asked plaintively.

'When I am ready. Good night.'

'But at least you will inspect the room, to see if everything is to your liking?' Churan demanded.

Lall turned her head and said something to him in their own hissing, guttural speech. She turned back. 'Just as you wish, then, Mr. Naismith. We will talk again in the morning.'

The three aliens crossed the lounge and entered their own room. The door slid shut after them.

Naismith paused a moment, listening: he could hear Lall and Churan moving about in their room, talking sleepily together, with occasional bursts of acrimony. There was no point in waiting any longer. Naismith moved noiselessly out into the corridor. The drifting red trail guided his feet; at the first turning, he deliberately left it. He went down a flight of stairs, stepped through a narrow doorway, and found himself in darkness relieved only by spectral, phosphorescent glows from the outlines of machinery here and there. He kept moving down the narrow aisle, under a low ceiling, not pausing to examine any of the machines he passed. For the moment all he wanted was to put distance between himself and the three aliens.

After a quarter of an hour, even the phosphorescent markings thinned out and ceased. He was groping in total darkness, thoroughly lost in the interior of the great ship.

Satisfied that he was secure for the moment, Naismith sat down in the darkness and considered his position. In spite of its immense, almost overwhelming implications, the problem was basically that of buyer against seller. Each party had something the other wanted, and each was determined to give as little as possible. Naismith's first objective was to keep the aliens from coercing him: that was now accomplished, since he was out of their reach. His next objective must be to improve his bargaining position. That meant, above all, increasing his knowledge: for it was knowledge that Lall and Churan held out as bait, and knowledge again that gave them a tactical superiority. His course, therefore, was clear. He must begin by exploring the ship, no matter how many weeks or even months—

The thought broke off. A breath of danger was passing down the narrow corridor, making his skin prickle and his nostrils widen. He stared blindly into the darkness: was the shadow-egg, invisible and intangible, passing there?

Whatever it was, in a moment it was gone. Naismith rose and once more began feeling his way down the corridor.

Hours later, he found a narrow passage leading off at right angles, and crossed the waist of the ship, emerging finally in a huge, deserted salon. Here the moving overhead lights followed him again, but there were no red trails on the floor, and he guessed that Lall and Churan had never been in this area.

In the days that followed, Naismith prowled the empty ship alone. Its gigantic scale never ceased to oppress and astonish him: it was impossible to imagine what kind of people could have built a vessel like this, equipped it so massively and elaborately, and then left it to be mounded over on the Colorado plain.

Wherever he went, the lights winked on ahead, winked off behind. There must be some way of illuminating whole rooms at once, but Naismith had not found it. He moved in a moving circle of pale light, while all around him was green silence. There were cyclopean galleries and choirs, around which he crawled like a fly; there were baths, gymnasia, theaters, game rooms, machine rooms, all empty with an inexpressible emptiness, hollow, not-quite-echoing....

Never once did he catch a glimpse of the aliens or their shadow-egg, although he felt sure they were trying to find him. Everywhere he went, there were enigmatic, silent machines including some that he guessed were television instruments, but he could not make them function. Here and there he saw symbols printed on the walls; they were in an alphabet resembling the Cyrillic, but with many added characters. Nowhere could he find a deck plan of the ship, a directory, a travel booklet, anything that would give him the least clue to the object of his search.

At last, on the fourth day, entirely by accident, he found it.

He was in a room filled with the omnipresent balloon-like armchairs and with tall, angular devices, chest high, on which square greenish plates of metal were arranged in two slanting, overlapping rows, forming an inverted V. They might have been magazine racks, with the thick metal plates substituting for magazines. As the thought came, Naismith put his hand casually on one of them, and the thing flapped open with a clatter. Crouched, ready to fight or run, he stared at it.

The rank of overlapping plates had opened, exposing the whole face of one of the plates: and where a blank square of greenish metal should have been, he saw a moving, brilliantly colored picture.

Naismith's breathing quickened. He hardly heard the voice which spoke casually and incomprehensibly from the machine. This was it; he had found it: this was the library.

The picture he was watching showed a woman in an oddly cut red garment, posturing before a background of vaguely Oriental domes that gleamed in bright sunshine. The picture changed; now he was looking at a passageway between earth-colored buildings, down which men in white robes walked with heads bowed. It might almost have been a street scene in ancient Turkey or Egypt, except that the men were leading bright blue, hairless beasts of burden. ...

The picture changed again. Now, under a gigantic orange sun, stick-thin brown creatures with many legs were building a scaffold of wooden rods. Naismith understood that he was being shown an interstellar travelogue: ports of call at which this very ship had touched, perhaps ... He watched until the pictures stopped, then closed the machine, opened it at a different place.

A new picture sprang into being: this time he saw two men, with thin, bearded faces, demonstrating some sort of physical apparatus. There was a thing that looked a little like a Crookes tube, and what might have been a series of accumulators. He could not understand a word of the spoken commentary, though the language sounded hauntingly familiar. The subject, at least, was apparently unrelated to the previous one. The arrangement, then, was either random or alphabetical, with a strong probability of the latter ... all he had to do was to find the key to it.

That took him two more days. Then his progress was rapid. The written language was a much modified English, phoneticized, with a simplified grammar and many vocabulary changes. The spoken language was more difficult, so slurred and elided that it was almost impossible to follow, but Naismith found he could neglect it by concentrating on reference codes which produced displays of printed books, page by page. By the end of his fourth day in the library, he had an accurate conception of the world these star-travelers had inhabited.

He had found out two things of importance, and another of possible significance. First, the entries under 'Time

Energy' in the library showed that the state of the art had not advanced since his own era; in fact, the temporal energy generator was regarded as a toy. There was no possibility, therefore, of his discovering another shadow-egg aboard the ship or being able to construct one: that invention was still to come.

Second, the Lenlu Om – Lall's people – were natives of a planet of 82 Eridani, and had been introduced into the Solar System in about the year 11,000. They were not called by that name, but the characteristics of those shown in the pictures were unmistakable.

Third, the framed pictures Naismith found on the walls, in places where Lall and Churan had apparently never been, were paintings and stereographs of Terrestrial scenes, including a number of portraits. The people represented, like those in the library machines, were ordinary native Terrestrials, in no way remarkable to Naismith's eye except for their costumes.

As far as Naismith could tell, pictures were missing from their frames wherever the aliens had gone. It was conceivable that this was simply the result of looting, but Naismith did not think it likely. The aliens seemed indifferent to all the other articles of value around them in the ship, and had apparently taken nothing from the world of 1980. It was Naismith's tentative opinion that something in the pictures was distasteful to Lall and Churan – that they had taken them down, and very likely destroyed them, in order to be rid of an unpleasant reminder.

Naismith sat up in bed. The room lights slowly came on as he did so, showing the unfamiliar walls paneled in magenta and apple green. As usual, he had worked in the library until he felt it unwise any longer to ignore his increasing fatigue; then he had chosen a new suite of rooms – there were hundreds, in this section of the ship alone, and he never used the same one twice – prepared and eaten his dinner, and gone to bed. But the thought that had come to him was so radical, so breathtaking—

In all the time he had spent aboard the ship, although he had many times wondered what had become of its passengers and crew, it had never once occurred to him to look for any personal possessions they might have left behind. The spotless, orderly appearance of everything in the ship had made him assume unconsciously that the rooms had been cleaned out and set in order when its passengers left.

And yet he knew that this ship cleaned and tidied itself. Dust deposited anywhere in a room slowly crept toward the nearest baseboard gutter, where it ran into channels – Naismith had traced them in the narrow passages behind the walls – leading to storage bins and, Naismith guessed, eventually to conversion chambers. Clothing taken from a closet and dropped on the floor would slowly, over the course of a few hours, creep back to its proper place, shedding its dirt in the process. Even the trails of sticky pigment Lall and Churan had left to guide them around the ship must have to be renewed every few days. And therefore—

Naismith swung himself out of bed in mounting excitement. Having examined a few of the wall closets in these living suites and found them empty, he had lost interest in them. But some of the bedrooms – this one, for example – had clothing in their closets!

He cursed his own stupidity. If clothing were part of the rooms' standard equipment, as he had unthinkingly assumed, why would some rooms have it and not others? But if this room had been occupied at the time the ship made its final landing, and if the occupant had left his clothing behind, then it was an almost foregone conclusion that he had left other possessions as well.

Naismith went straight to the largest wall panel, thumbed the control strip to open it, found it empty. He tried the smaller, cubical one on the adjoining wall.

At first it seemed equally empty; then he saw a scrap of paper or foil on the bottom of the compartment. He drew it out. Printed on the foil in luminous purple letters were the words, 'GIGANTIC ALL-NIGHT GALA! Dancing! Sensorials! Prizes! Y Section ballroom, beginning 23 hours

30, 12th day of Khair ...' followed by a date which Naismith translated as 11,050.

It was little enough in itself, but Naismith clutched it as if it were precious. He went on from one wall to another, searching out panels and opening them. But the results were disappointing: a plastic identity card made out in the name of Isod Rentro, and bearing the stereo picture of a man's lean, foxy face; a bundle of metallo-plastic tokens strung on a wire; and a toy of some sort, a gray plastic box with a tiny viewscreen.

Absently Naismith pressed the button on the side of the box. The viewscreen lighted up, and he was looking into the pale, lean face of the man on the identity card. A voice began to speak – a nasal, negligent, cultured voice. Naismith caught a few words, recognized them as a date a few weeks earlier than the one on the 'all-night gala' announcement.

He set the box down with reverent care. He had had an incredible piece of luck, and had almost failed to recognize it. He was looking at the journal of Isod Rentro, a passenger aboard this ship in the year of our Lord 11,050.

Rentro was dressed in a loose-fitting blouse of metallic silver-white, with a violet scarf at his throat. His skin was pale and unhealthy-looking, very faintly freckled, as if it had seldom been exposed to the sun. His hands were thin. He gestured wearily with a long, carved holder in which a green stick of something was smoldering.

The scene flicked, changed. Naismith was looking out at a vast space in which crowds of colorfully dressed people moved, while Rentro's commentary continued. He was looking, Naismith realized, at the spaceship's berth before the takeoff. Another ship was visible in the distance, under the dome of a gigantic transparent roof. Music was playing; colored streamers were twisting through the air.

A chime sounded, and Naismith saw faces turn, hands begin to wave. Like an elevator dropping, the whole vast concourse slowly began to drift downward. Above, the transparent roof parted, opened out into two graceful wings. They, too, drifted downward and out of sight.

Naismith had a glimpse of a misty landscape, quickly and silently shrinking. Clouds whipped past and were gone. The horizon grew round, then the earth assumed the shape of a bowl, a sphere, visibly dwindling. The sky grew purple, then black; stars appeared.

The screen flickered again. Rentro came into view once more, still sitting calmly in his cabin, with an expression of amused boredom. He spoke a few final words, gestured, and the screen went dark.

It lighted again immediately. Rentro appeared, dressed in a different costume, against a background Naismith recognized. He caught his breath involuntarily. This was a place he knew – the great lounge at the end of this section, the one with the enormous central chandelier and the tiers of balconies.

Walls, furniture, everything was exactly the same: but the vast room was brilliantly lit, aswarm with people. It was like watching a corpse suddenly grow vividly, beautifully alive.

Rentro turned, faced the screen, spoke a few words. A young woman in a white gown came into view; her complexion was rosy, her eyes surrounded by startling blue rings of cosmetics. Rentro took her casually by the arm, spoke her name – Izel Dormay – and added a few words which made them both smile. The view changed again....

Naismith followed the record through the first few weeks of the voyage. Allowing for the difference in technology and in the incredible consumption-level of these people, it was very much like a luxury cruise of the twentieth century. The passengers played games, watched the entertainment screens, ate, drank, strolled about. Once or twice a ship's officer appeared, spoke a few polite words into the screen. The crew and most of the passengers were human, but Naismith occasionally glimpsed members of Lall's race.

Then there was a change. It happened so gradually that Naismith was not aware of it at first. The crowds in the lounges and game rooms grew less. Crew members in their gray and black uniforms were more in evidence, and moved more purposefully. Once Naismith saw a stumbling, slack-jawed man being helped out of a room by two crewmen: he looked drunken or perhaps drugged. Rentro's commentary was disdainfully cool, as usual, but Naismith caught a worried expression on his face.

A day or so later, there was no mistaking the difference. Few people were in the lounges or on the promenades. Rentro ventured out briefly, then went back to his cabin; his next entry in the journal was made there, and so were all those that followed. His expression grew daily more strained: he looked, Naismith thought, like a badly frightened man. Once he made a long speech into the machine, which Naismith would have given much to interpret, but he could only catch a word here and there, no matter how often he played it over – 'carrying', 'danger', 'contagion'.

A day later, the entry was brief, and Naismith was able to make it out: 'We are returning to Earth.'

The rest of the journal consisted of brief entries, only the date and a few perfunctory words, with two exceptions. In the first, Rentro spoke at some length, seriously and soberly, from time to time consulting a tablet he held in his hand: it occurred to Naismith that he was making his will.

The second time, after announcing the date and repeating a phrase he had used several times before, Rentro suddenly and horrifyingly lost his composure. With a distorted, writhing face, he shouted something into the machine – four words, of which Naismith could make out only one. It was 'Greenskins' – the contemporary name for Lall's people.

Two days after that, the journal stopped. It simply ended, without any clue to what had happened next.

Naismith searched the adjoining suites, then and on the following day, and found three more such personal journals. When he had run them all off he was no wiser: all told essentially the same story, and all ended abruptly, at varying times, before the ship reached Earth.

For the time being, he gave it up. Naismith had been two weeks alone in the ship, enduring its green silences, and the solitude was beginning to wear on him. He began to think of going back to the aliens. He had explored the ship as thoroughly as he could, in the limits of the time he had spent, and without going near the red trails left by Lall and Churan.

It occurred to him for the first time that this precaution might have been unnecessary.

Suppose the aliens had begun to use the time machine to search for him as soon as they had found him missing. Almost certainly they would have begun by searching their own lounge and the corridor outside it, for a month or so into the future. If they had done that, *and found him*, there would never have been any necessity to search elsewhere in the ship. Accordingly, if Naismith was in fact *going to be found* in the aliens' suite or near it, he could roam anywhere he pleased until that time, elsewhere in the ship, without any fear of discovery.

It was a curious sensation, following the fading red trail on the carpet. Here and there still fainter trails branched off. Doubtless the aliens had first explored the ship at random, as he himself had done; these early trails led nowhere. But the strong red trail, recently renewed, meant that there were places in the ship the aliens wanted to revisit. What were they?

The path led through empty galleries and lounges, down a broad corridor, up a stair ... Naismith's own knowledge of the ship soon failed him; he no longer knew where he was except in a general sense.

He passed through an anteroom into a vast, echoing natatorium surrounded by balconies. Cushions and reclining chairs were strewn beside the pool; the tank itself was filled with clear water. There was no debris on the bottom, not a particle of dust visible on the surface. Remembering the colorful crowds he had seen in Rentro's journal, Naismith was oppressed by the sense of their almost-living presence – as if they had only stepped into the next room for a moment. ...

Beyond the natatorium was a row of dressing rooms, and beyond that, unexpectedly, a small gymnasium. Here, for the first time, there was evidence of an alien presence. The parallel bars, horses, trampolines had been pushed aside, and three small black-metal boxes lay in the middle of the polished floor. One had a line of transparencies and dials on its upper face. Remembering the machine the aliens had used on him in their Los Angeles apartment, Naismith was careful not to approach them. He skirted the room cautiously, looking for a continuation of the red trail, but there was none: it ended here.

He turned. And Churan was standing in the doorway, with a black, lensed machine on a tripod beside him.

With shock tingling through his nervous system, Naismith took a step forward; the machine swiveled slightly on its mounting to follow him. He stopped.

'Don't do it, Naismith,' Churan said tensely. 'This is a force gun, locked onto you as its target. If I press the release—' he showed Naismith a tiny control box in his hand – 'or if you move too suddenly, the gun will fire.'

Naismith forced himself to relax. 'Why the armament?' he asked contemptuously.

'We have decided it is safer. If you have no plan to attack us, it will make no difference to you. Now follow, please, and make no sudden moves for your own safety.'

He backed away, and the machine rolled back beside him, its glittering lenses swiveling to stare at Naismith, almost with an air of intelligence: as if the machine were alive, watching him. ...

I should have looked for the arsenal, Naismith thought, with a sick feeling of defeat. *But perhaps it would not have made any difference – they would have found me there before I could take anything ...*

Churan backed out into the middle of the corridor and stopped. The headband with its metal box lay on the carpet. 'Pick it up,' he ordered curtly.

Naismith moved forward as slowly as he dared. 'Where are Lall and the child?' he asked, temporizing.

'Safe,' Churan spat. 'Pick up the headband!'

Naismith stooped, got the thing in his fingers. 'Tell me,

Churan,' he said, 'why all this caution? Why can't you just go forward in time and see if everything turns out all right?'

Churan's amber eyes gleamed. 'We did that, Mr. Naismith. The results – were ambiguous. We decided to take no chances with you. Put on the headband.'

Naismith raised the headband, weighing it in his hands. He swayed slightly, watching the feral head of the machine turn, almost imperceptibly, on its oiled socket. What was the principle involved? Heat? If he could somehow manage to reduce his body temperature—

Churan glared. 'Put it on!'

Naismith's body tensed. For reasons he could not clearly understand, the thing he held was intensely abhorrent. It might be better to jump, take his chances—

'I warn you!' said Churan, holding the control box in squat fingers.

Naismith's lips pulled back in a grimace. He raised the headband, slowly fitted it over his skull.

The last thing he saw, before darkness crashed around him, was Churan's triumphant smile.

9

His head ached. He was sitting on the floor, holding his head in his hands to quiet the throbbing pain. He looked around, moving with exaggerated caution, for the slightest motion made his head feel as if it were about to split.

The headband lay across the room, bent out of shape. Churan was staring at him, breathing hard, sweat was beaded on his narrow forehead.

'How do you feel?' he asked hoarsely.

Naismith tried to sit up, groaned and slumped back. 'Pain in my head,' he answered indistinctly. 'What happened?'

'You tore off the helmet halfway through,' Churan muttered. 'It's lucky for you that I had neutralized the gun. Make no mistake – it's locked on again now!' he twitched, and resumed, 'I don't understand how— You are not supposed to be able to resume voluntary control until after the memory unit has stopped working. ... Do you understand everything I say?'

'Why shouldn't I?' Naismith asked, and then halted, transfixed by a realization that almost drove his pain into the background.

He and Churan were not speaking English. They were talking in the language of his dreams – the same hissing, guttural tongue the aliens used – but now every word was clear.

'Who is the Highborn?' Churan demanded, inching nearer.

'The hereditary aristarch,' Naismith answered impatiently. 'She—' Once more he stopped, in total dismay. The knowledge that he found in his mind, a complete and detailed history of the Highborn and her court, had not been there before.

'The process was successful, then,' Churan said with evident relief. 'You missed the end of the disk, of course, but we can supply that later, if necessary. I was afraid that— Sit still until you feel better.' He turned, retreated.

He was back in a moment, followed by Lall. Both aliens were staring at him with an air of suppressed excitement. Churan, muttering something under his breath, stepped over to the wall and picked up the damaged headband, showing it to Lall.

Her muddy complexion paled. She held out her hand for the headband, fingered the bent metal unbelievingly. 'He did that? While the educator was turned on?'

Both aliens stared at Naismith. 'Does he have the compulsion?'

'Obviously not.'

Lall snarled at him, 'How do you *know*?'

The pain in Naismith's head had eased a little. He got

gingerly to his feet and retreated with cautious movements to the wall. He leaned back, watching and listening, while the aliens erupted into a sudden furious argument.

'How, then?' Churan demanded, thrusting his face into Lall's. 'Tell me how.'

'Try it yourself!' she returned, and thrust the headband into his hand.

Churan looked at it with surprise; his amber eyes narrowed, then glinted with understanding.

'The disk will begin at the moment it was interrupted,' Lall said. 'Go ahead, put it on – what harm can it do *you*?'

Churan grinned mirthlessly. 'True. Very well.' He pried dubiously at the bent framework. 'I do not know if it will function—' He shrugged and put the headband on. His eyes closed then opened again.

'Well?' the woman demanded.

Churan took the headband off slowly. 'You were right. The compulsion formula was almost all there – he could have heard only the first syllable of it.'

Again the two aliens stared at him, with something like respect in their faces.

'This changes matters,' Churan muttered. He glanced sidelong at Naismith, and added, 'Don't forget, he understands what we say now. Come—' He took Lall's arm, drew her aside.

Naismith straightened up. 'Just a moment!' he said. 'Are you going to go on trying to keep me in the dark? Because if so, I give you warning now that my cooperation is over.' He gestured at the gun on its tripod. 'Turn that thing off, and tell me what the machine was meant to do.'

The aliens looked at him sullenly: 'There was a compulsion formula in it,' Lall said at last, 'to make sure you would do as we wish, when you are past the Barrier.'

Naismith said, 'Then the story you told me about myself was false?'

'No, it was true, every word,' said Churan earnestly, coming forward a step. 'We only wanted to make sure—'

'Wait,' Lall interrupted. She peered into Naismith's face.

'Mr. Naismith – do you hate the Lenlu Din?'

Naismith opened his mouth to reply, then shut it again. At her words, memories had begun to swim up out of some black place in his mind.

'The Lenlu Din ...' he said. Plump, floating people in puffed costumes of scarlet and gold, peach, frost-white, orchid, buff. Shrill overbearing voices, glittering eyes. ...

'This may be the answer,' the woman was saying in a tense undertone to Churan. 'Forget the compulsion – if he really hates them, he will do it because he wants to. Let us try him on the lie detector. What can we lose now?'

Churan looked uncertainly at Naismith, and there was a flicker of anger in his eyes. 'How can I tell?' he muttered. 'He is a Shefth.'

'All the more reason. We will do it. Come.' She beckoned to Naismith, started off down the corridor.

'The gun,' said Naismith, not moving.

'No,' she said. 'We are going to be frank with you, Mr. Naismith – but the gun stays, a little longer.'

Naismith shrugged and followed. The gun retreated as he moved, rolling smoothly along beside the two aliens, with its lensed muzzle trained steadily on him.

It was that way all the way back to the aliens' suite. The pain in Naismith's head was receding, only a dull ache now, but his mind was confused by an insistent crowd of images, sounds, voices babbling together, faces that were unknown and yet familiar ...

Yet he was dimly aware that there was something unexplained about what had just happened. Why had Churan found him just *there*, in the corridor outside the gymnasium? ...

They entered the lounge, where Yegga sprang up from the floor, spilling a bowl of something greenish-yellow, and went to its mother with an angry squall.

She cuffed it aside impatiently. 'Sit down, Mr. Naismith. Gunda, get the detector.'

'It will take a few—' Churan began. 'No, I am wrong, I

have to retrieve the time vehicle anyway. I may as well do it, and then—'

'Go, get it,' she said impatiently. Churan went out, with a last sullen glance at Naismith.

Naismith lowered himself into a chair, thinking hard. Lall sat down opposite him, her long amber eyes hooded and watchful. 'What were you doing in the ship, all that time until Gunda found you?' she demanded.

Naismith stared back at her somberly. Twice now, he was thinking, someone had tried to tamper with his mind – first Wells, now Churan – and twice, while he was unconscious, something in him had exploded with incredible violence ... some *thing* buried in his mind. Naismith felt the birth of an angry impatience. This must not go on; sooner or later he must find a way to reach those buried depths, force them to give up their knowledge....

'I was in the library,' he answered.

Lall's fingers curled tensely on the table. 'And what did you find there?'

She was so evidently nervous, anxious about his reply ... Naismith considered her narrowly, and said, 'I found out that the time vehicle is not a part of this era's technology.'

Her body visibly relaxed. She laughed. 'I could have told you that much, Mr. Naismith. No, if you are going to build your own time vehicle, you cannot do it here. For that we must take you many centuries forward.'

'How far?'

She shook her head. 'When the time comes, Mr. Naismith.'

Churan came in, carrying the machine under one arm and an oblong gray case in the other. He set the gray case down on the table, with a curt 'Here', and crossed the room to deposit the other machine in the wall cabinet.

Lall was removing the cover from the oblong box, revealing a smooth gray-metal base with two protrusions – one a dull pinkish-gray ovoid, the other a more complex shape, somewhat like a misshapen mushroom.

'This is an ordinary lie detector, Mr. Naismith,' Lall said, pushing it toward him. She moved her chair quickly, stood up and stepped back. Churan was at the farther wall, watching intently. The gun on its tripod pointed steadily at him.

'Try it,' said Lall. 'Pick up a dish in one hand, take the grip of the machine in the other. ... Now say, "I am not holding the dish."'

Naismith followed directions. Nothing happened.

'Now say, "I am holding the dish."'

Naismith repeated it after her. The oval bulb flared into pink, hot brightness.

'Now this is all you have to do,' Lall said breathlessly. 'Put your hand on that grip and say to me, "I hate the Lenlu Din."'

Churan moved his hand slightly: in it was the control box of the automatic gun.

Naismith stiffened, aware that he had let the crisis find him unready. If he refused, he would be shot. If he took the test, and failed—

Once more the images of those bright, bloated people drifted up to the surface of his mind. He examined his own feelings dispassionately. He neither hated nor loved them. To part of his mind they were utterly strange; to another part, they were familiar and almost commonplace....

'Now, Mr. Naismith,' said Lall sharply.

Naismith put his hand on the rounded mushroom-top of the grip. It was a shape that smoothly fitted his palm. He tensed his muscles, without hope – he knew he could not move fast enough to escape the gun. Because he could think of nothing else to do, he said, 'I hate the Lenlu Din.'

The oval bulb burned fiercely for a long moment, then slowly faded, glimmered, went out. Naismith heard Lall's and Churan's intake of breath, saw them relax and begin to move toward the table.

He stared blankly at the detector, thinking, *But that's impossible!*

The staggering thing was that the aliens themselves showed no suspicion. As far as they were concerned, the detector test was obviously conclusive. Lall said briskly, 'One more day here will be enough. You will put on the educator headband once more – without tricks, this time, Mr. Naismith. Then it will take you some twelve hours to absorb all you have learned ... the process is sometimes fatiguing, and it is important that you rest during that period. After that,' she finished, 'you will be ready to begin building your time vehicle.'

Naismith looked at her sharply, but there was no humor in her expression. 'Do you mean that literally?' he demanded. 'I thought—'

'How else can we get you into the City?' she countered. 'You may be positive they will check whatever story you tell. If you say you materialized in the factory city of Ul in the fifth century before the Founding, they will go there in their own time vehicle to see. Therefore, you must not only tell the story, you must actually be there, building that vehicle, when they come to look. It will take you a little over ten years.'

'Ten *years*,' said Naismith, stunned by the matter-of-factness in her tone.

'Understand this,' she said harshly, leaning toward him. 'It's that or nothing. Make up your mind.'

Her glance was sullen. Churan, across the room, was looking at him with the same expression, his eyes hooded and dull.

Naismith shrugged. 'What choice do I have?' He held out his hand. 'Give me the headband.'

... Afterwards, he lay back in a soft chair, his mind a cloudy confusion of new thoughts and images, while the three aliens prepared a meal and ate it.

'We are going to bed now,' Lall said dully to Naismith. 'Your room is there. Till the morning, then.'

They went into their room and closed the door. Naismith sat where he was for a while, then went to the room Lall had pointed out, examined the door controls. There was nothing unusual about them as far as he could determine; the door closed and opened again easily.

He went inside and lay down on the bed, half aware of his surroundings as the stream of memories, voices, faces came and went in his mind. When an hour had passed, he sat up.

He rose, opened the door and listened. There was no sound from the aliens' room. He closed the door behind him and moved quietly across the lounge. Outside, he followed the red trail, heading directly for the place where Churan had found him a few hours ago.

He passed through the natatorium again, into the gymnasium ... and stared with speculative interest at the pieces of equipment lying on the polished floor. Something had been prepared for him here: but what?

He moved closer, bent to examine the black case with the transparencies and dials. It was evidently the control box; three of the dials were calibrated and set. A fourth had only two positions, marked by a red dot and a white one. The pointer lay on the white dot.

Caution held him back, but Naismith had a sense that there were too many things still hidden in the background. Events were sweeping him on, and ignorance was still his most dangerous weakness. Certain risks had to be accepted.

He made up his mind. Kneeling, he turned the dial from white to red, then got to his feet and stepped back.

Not quickly enough.

The far end of the gymnasium darkened suddenly. Out of that blackness, like a vault opening where the far wall should have been, something stirred.

Fear entered the room. It came like a cold wind out of that darkness. Naismith's fingers were cold; his skin prickled. Straining his eyes, he could make out a glint of light here, another there, as something impossibly huge came toward him in the blackness. It was the monster of his dream! Two little red eyes stared at him, and there was a faint rattle of bony plates. The head of the thing began to emerge into the light ...

Naismith forced himself to remain still as that immense body came fully into view. It was a shape of tremendous animal power, armored and clawed, many-limbed ... but the most frightening thing about it was the look of intelligence, of merciless, ancient wisdom in its eyes....

With a bone-chilling roar, the thing sprang. In spite of himself, Naismith flinched back. The gigantic body swelled, filled the universe . . and was gone. The darkness winked out. The gymnasium wall reappeared.

Naismith found himself trembling and covered with sweat.

The far wall darkened again. With a sense of panic, Naismith realized that the experience was beginning once more. Again the stirring in the darkness, again the red eyes, the emergence: but this time the beast sprang more quickly. The lights came up; after a moment, the darkness fell a third time. Grimly, Naismith watched the same terrifying bulk appear even more quickly, spring with less delay. A fourth time, and a fifth, he watched, before the lights came on and stayed on: the cycle was over.

And that, he thought bleakly, *was probably only the beginning. The beast itself must move incomparably faster than that ...*

He left the gymnasium and went into the corridor where Churan had found him before. Almost absent-mindedly, he glanced around. His attention sharpened, as he thought again of the anomaly of Churan's finding him just *here.* Why not in the gymnasium itself? Why in the corridor outside?

A little farther down the corridor there was an open doorway. Naismith remembered glancing in before, and finding only a small, uninteresting room. He went over to it, looked in again. It was as he recalled it, a tiny green room, hardly larger than a closet.

He stood in the doorway, frowning. There was a small bare desk, the same green as the walls, a simple-looking vision instrument over it, and an array of green and white panels on the wall behind.

The little room might have been a storeroom of some kind: but it was the wrong size. Either it should have been much bigger, Naismith thought, or else there should have been no desk, no vision apparatus. In sudden excitement, he rounded the desk, began to fumble at the control strips of the panels. This might, just might, be the purser's office, with all the records of the voyage...

But it was not. It was the dispensary.

The wall panels held rack on rack of drugs in cylindrical bottles, each elaborately labeled. Probably most of them were worthless by now. Naismith examined a few, put them back. He tried another section of the wall.

Inside were gleaming, ranked strips of metal, each labeled with a name and a date. Naismith touched one experimentally, and it tilted out into his hand, a metal-bound sheaf of papers.

It was the case-history of a passenger aboard the ship: the others were the same.

In five minutes the whole story lay under his hands. A virus carried by the greenskinned people had mutated; the new form attacked *homo sapiens*. The symptoms were fever, nausea and intense feelings of anxiety, followed by collapse and coma, then a slow recovery. Death ensued in only a small percentage of cases: but every recovered victim had suffered severe and irreparable brain damage. There were stereo pictures, from which Naismith averted his eyes: vacant faces, dull eyes, jaws hanging....

The epidemic had broken out on the same day the ship left Earth. In the end, it must have been only the greenskins, immune to their own infection, who had been able to bring the ship back and land it safely with its cargo of mindless human beings. And all over Earth, the same tragedy...

Naismith could imagine the shambling aments who had been the luxury ship's passengers, wandering out onto the plain by ones and twos ... out into a land where nothing waited for them but death by exposure and starvation...

Naismith closed the book slowly and put it back in its place.

He understood now why this was a so-called 'dead period'. Only a handful of immune human beings must have survived, along with the greenskins, to rebuild civilization slowly and painfully over the course of centuries. Yes, that explained many things....

10

In the morning, both aliens were sullen and heavy-eyed; they spoke to each other in monosyllables, and to Naismith not at all. The child, Yegga, alternately screamed and whined.

After they had breakfasted, Lall and Churan seemed to come sluggishly to life. The woman began to dress in the same short robe she had worn yesterday, saying over her shoulder to Naismith, 'Today you will train in the gymnasium – there is some equipment there which will prepare you to hunt Zug.'

'I know. I found it there.'

She turned to look at him expressionlessly, then went on with her dressing. 'Very well, that will save us time. You saw the Zug, then? What did you think of it?'

'Very impressive, but I don't see why it was necessary.'

'You are to play the role of a Zug hunter,' she said, fastening the robe around her waist. 'If you should see one without preparation, you would betray yourself immediately.'

'I see.' Remembering the vision that had come to him that night in his Beverly Hills apartment, Naismith asked, 'And the gun? What was that for?'

She turned with a questioning expression. Churan, who had just entered the lounge carrying the time vehicle, paused to listen. 'Gun?' asked Lall.

'Yes, certainly,' Naismith answered with a touch of impatience. 'That night, in my bedroom. Tell me, just what would have happened if I had accepted that gun?'

The two aliens looked at each other. Churan opened his mouth to speak, but Lall said sharply, 'Be still!' She turned to Naismith, fumbling in the pocket of her robe, and produced a black cylinder. She pushed bowls and plates aside, and rapidly sketched a pistol recognizable as the one Naismith had seen, with its flowing lines and massive grip. Churan came to watch over her shoulder; there was something strained in his silent attention.

'Was it a gun like this?' she asked.

'Yes, of course.'

She turned away indifferently, putting the cylinder back in her pocket. 'It would have given you a compulsion to kill Zug,' she said. 'Only a precaution.'

Churan was staring at her silently. 'Well, are you ready?' she snapped at him. 'Why do we have to wait – why can't we go?'

Churan shrugged, held up the machine in both hands. He touched the controls; the shadow-egg sprang into being around him. With a last quick glance to left and right, Lall herded the child inside, stood back for Naismith to enter, stepped in herself.

It was more crowded than ever in the shadow-egg, and the scent of the aliens' bodies was oppressively heavy. By their tense attitudes and their sidelong glances at him, Naismith could tell that his presence made them equally uneasy. Seated on the stool, Churan touched the controls, and they drifted up from the floor, across the lounge and into the corridor. Once more they followed the red line; blackness swallowed them as they passed through the mound, then they were in dazzling sunlight.

Suddenly, the contrast between the unpleasant closeness of the shadow-egg and that clean brightness outside was more than Naismith could stand.

'Wait,' he said. 'I want to get out.'

'What?' Lall and Churan stared at him.

'Set me down there, on top of the mound,' he said, pointing. 'I want to breathe the fresh air for a minute.'

Churan said impatiently. 'We have no time to waste – you

can breathe where you are.' He put his hands on the controls, but Lall stopped him.

'After all, you want to practice using the ejector,' she muttered. 'What harm can it do? Set him down.'

Churan grumbled, but in a moment the shadow-egg swung up along the steep slope, rose to the summit and hovered there, a few inches above the grasstops.

Churan stared down at the machine in his lap, rubbing his squat fingers together and grunting. At last he said, 'Miko, move back a little – take the child. Mr. Naismith, you stay where you are.'

The woman and child crowded back beside Churan. Naismith waited tensely. Churan's fingers touched the controls again, and abruptly Naismith felt himself picked up, swung out away from the aliens. The shadow-egg had bulged outward; now it was like two eggs, connected by a narrow tube of shadow. Then, without warning, the bulge vanished. Naismith was falling. . . .

He landed with a jar, arms out for balance. When he looked up, the shadow-egg was drifting off on a long slant down toward the base of the mound.

He stood looking around him, breathing painfully deep. The greenish-yellow plain rolled away unbroken to the horizon. It was early, the sun low in the east, and the thick grasses around his legs were beaded with dew. The sun was warm, but the air had a bracing coolness. Naismith filled his lungs again and again; earth smells, green smells, scents of spring flowers.

He sat down and watched the great wrinkled sheet of cloud drift slowly toward the west. Down below, the shadow-egg still hovered over the plain, a hundred yards or so away. He could just make out Lall's and Churan's faces: they seemed close in conversation. Farther out, a flock of birds arose from the grass and settled again. Still farther away, Naismith saw a larger body moving through the grassy hummocks – a quadruped, too large for a deer; perhaps an elk. But there were no men. Not a thread of smoke; not a cloud of dust.

From this height, he could see the immense buried shape of the ship more plainly. The world around him was peaceful and empty, as if waiting for another Creation.

Naismith thought of the blank thirty-one years of his life, and of his four years in California, now seen as futile and misunderstood; then of the tremendous distance he had traveled in the shadow-egg with Lall and Churan – over nine thousand years; and the Earth was still here with its seasons.

He thought of the distance he had yet to go – 'twenty thousand years, Mr. Naismith,' Churan had said. And it seemed to him, as it had from the beginning, that there was a monstrous meaning hidden in all this. It was all around him, in the slow drift of the clouds across the sky, in the sense of the buried giant under his feet. For the first time, he felt less as if he were fighting a battle than as if he were engaged in a quest for knowledge.

He stood up again. *Who am I?* he thought; and unexpectedly, his body began to tremble. Images floated up into awareness: he could see the corridors of the City, and the colorful, floating throngs of Lenlu Din – all clear but distant, like figures in a peepshow. He knew who the Shefthi were, and could even conjure up some of their faces ... but there was no image of himself. Who and what was he? ... that was what he had to find out.

He stared down at the shadow-egg. The two aliens were still talking together, but in a moment they glanced up. Naismith gestured. Churan raised his hand; then the shadow-egg began to drift nearer, growing larger as it swept up the side of the mound. There was something incongruous about the egg's absolute internal stillness as it moved – as if the egg itself were really fixed, in some transcendent dimension, while the world swam under it.

The thought ended as the shadow-egg came to rest, near enough to touch. The orifice opened. 'Get in!' said Lall.

... Then he was inside, in the suffocating closeness of the shadow-egg, while the landscape receded beneath. They were rising, moving more and more swiftly northeastward; and Naismith saw that time outside was at a standstill: there was no movement of wind in the tall grasses below, and the clouds overhead were as solid and motionless as if painted on the sky.

'Where to now?' he asked.

The aliens glanced up but did not speak. Even the child, Yegga, was staring at him silently.

The Earth became a blurred green ball, spinning massively below. The sense of motion was so powerful that Naismith had an impulse to brace himself against it. But when he closed his eyes, there was no feeling of movement at all.

When the Earth's giddy motion slowed, Naismith saw a glint of silver ahead, and realized that they must be approaching one of the Great Lakes, probably Lake Michigan. Now they were dropping closer to the ground, skirting the rim of the lake ... slowly, now, almost at a walking pace ... The egg came to rest.

Churan's fingers touched the controls. Outside, day was abruptly replaced by night: then day again, like a sudden white blow. Night, day, night, blending now into a shivering grayness. Once more Naismith saw the sun arching over them like a fireball, and the ground below seemed to heave and then subside, while a mist of foliage came and went, came and went.

Abruptly, there were roads. They sprang into being as if die-stamped – real highways, crisscrossing the land. At the foot of the lake there was a blurred city, growing and changing too fast for Naismith to catch its outlines. There was an impression of mud-brown hovels, replaced instantly by taller, paler buildings; then skyscrapers were sprouting upward, glittering, like a sudden growth of crystals.

Now the growth stopped, fell back. In another moment the city was gone; the roads were gone: nothing was left but the bare earth and a scattering of tiny, cone-roofed structures no bigger than barrels.

'What's happened?' Naismith demanded.

'They went underground,' Lall said tonelessly. 'The city is still there.' A breath of darkness crossed the sky; there were glints of fiery light in it, gone almost too quickly to see. 'There was a war,' she added.

'Here?' Churan asked.

'A little farther,' the woman muttered.

Day again: night; day. And the shadow-egg was hovering, under a late-afternoon sky. It moved, drifting down toward the nearest of the cone-roofed objects. Naismith saw now that the thing was a ventilator.

The shadow-egg went on dropping. The ground came up around them like a tide of darkness, and Naismith held his breath instinctively as it mounted over their heads. There was an instant of stifling blackness, and then they were dropping down through a blue-green cavern ... a vast place, acres of gigantic machines under a rock ceiling, illuminated by the eye-hurting glare of mercury vapor lights. The place was gigantic, throbbing with power ... and empty.

Naismith looked around as the shadow-egg touched. 'Where are all the people?'

'Dead,' said Lall tensely. 'There was a war. They are all dead.' She moistened her lips. 'Now let me give you your instructions. You realize that once we have dropped you here, you are on your own. When you were thrown back in time, *this* is where you will say you landed. You will find here an unfinished time vehicle, the first crude prototype. You will complete it, following the plans you find beside it. Then you will go forward to the City. After you get through the Barrier, the rest is up to you.' The shadow-egg was drifting down a wide corridor between gigantic machines.

'There it is,' she said.

Naismith saw a clear space, some low workbenches, and leaning against the wall, a thing that might have been the skeleton of a rocket-sled. It was a tapered bar of metal, six feet long, with two crosspieces. Controls were set into the upper crosspiece, and Naismith could imagine the rider lying on the shaft, feet on the lower crosspiece, hands gripping the upper one like handlebars. ...

'That is the time machine?' he asked, half incredulously.

'No, not yet. It can be adapted as such. The inventors were trying to make a device for exploring the interior of the Earth. They hoped in this way to escape the devastation which overtook them. But all they succeeded in doing was to neutralize matter. If you boarded the machine as it now is, you would simply fall through the Earth, and go on falling. The propulsive unit is not installed.'

Naismith glanced around. Tools lay on the workbenches, among scattered papers, as if someone had laid them aside only an hour ago ... He felt a touch of uneasiness. 'What happened to them?' he asked.

'Killed in the first attack,' Lall said emotionlessly. That black cloud you saw, just before we stopped – that was the bombs.'

'How—?' began Naismith. But already Lall was drawing the child back beside her; Churan's fingers were busy on the controls. Naismith felt himself lifted as the shadow-egg bulged again. Then he was dropped unceremoniously on the stone floor. The shadow-egg hovered a few feet away.

'One thing she forgot to tell you,' said Churan, with an unpleasant smile. The *second* attack is going to take place in just thirty seconds. That is the one that pulverizes this City to the depth of fifty meters.'

It was like a pailful of icy water in the face. Naismith found himself thinking with cold clarity, *Then the workers must have gone down to shelter. That's why there are no bodies.*

'But why?' he said, taking a step closer. His mind was ferociously concentrated on the shadow-egg: he must succeed in getting back in, somehow ...

'You should not have told us about the gun, Mr. Naismith,' said Lall, watching him through narrowed eyes.

Realization struck him. The aliens had *not* sent the apparition of the gun. They had not sent the dreams, either. Then there were others, who—

'Ten seconds,' said Churan, glancing up from his controls.

'The lie detector—' said Naismith desperately.

'They know about you,' replied Lall. 'Therefore you are useless to us.' Her face went hard and ugly. 'The whole effort is wasted.'

'Five seconds,' added Churan. 'Four. Three . . .'

Naismith whirled. In one leap he reached the skeletal machine; feet and hands were on the crosspiece. He found a lever under his fingers, pulled it over hard.

The world went grayish and unreal around him. As it toppled, the machine began to sink into the floor – falling, as if the stone floor and the earth beneath it were so much mist.

Once more, before the darkness closed over his head, the last things he saw were the triumphant smiles of the aliens.

II

Naismith's first emotion was a consuming rage. Gathering himself, he kicked against the crossbar, flung his body upward – and was hurled back again by a curved, elastic wall. He landed hard against the metal framework, which began to revolve slowly and dizzyingly around him. The falling sensation continued.

His one opportunity was gone: for a moment that was all he could think of. If he had been able to leap out of the machine's field during the first second of his fall . . . but it was impossible to get out of the field without turning off the machine, as he had just discovered.

In fact, the opportunity had been illusory. He had been doomed from the moment he turned on the machine. Now he was falling, falling endlessly – to what fate?

The aliens had told him one truth and one lie; he had taken the lie for the truth, exactly as they had intended him to do.

Rage and despair all but choked him, as he clung to the metal framework, falling, in darkness and silence. He wanted to live!

A faint hope came, as his fingers touched the control

knobs on the crossbar. If the aliens had lied about this, too ... Cautiously he tried one knob after another, avoiding the lever which had turned the machine on. There was no perceptible result, except that, when he had turned the third knob, he felt a cool breath of air.

There was something he had not even considered: at least he would not smother on his way down. ... But he did not succeed in arresting his fall, or changing its direction, so far as he could tell, by a hair's breadth.

The thought of the gulf below him was hideous. What, actually, was happening to him at this moment? The answer came at once. He was acting out one of the oldest physics problems in the books, something that every freshman was familiar with – the imaginary tunnel drilled through the Earth.

In fact, his body was a harmonic oscillator. Assuming a homogeneous Earth and a non-rotating frame, he would describe a long, narrow ellipse around the Earth's center. His grip on the crossbar tightened convulsively. Of course – and unless friction retarded him too much, he would rise at the antipodal point to exactly the same level he had started from!

Wait, now – he had fallen from the floor of an underground chamber perhaps a hundred feet or so under the surface ... *Where was he going to come out?*

The moment the question occurred to him, he realized that it was of vital importance. He had entered the Earth near Lake Michigan, probably not far from the site of Chicago. If he went straight through the planet, he should come out somewhere in the Indian Ocean ... and Chicago, he was sure, was several hundred feet above sea level!

Wait a moment ... he was neglecting the rotation of the Earth; that would bring him out some distance westward of the antipodal point. How far depended on the period of his motion. ... Call the radius of the Earth four thousand miles – about twenty million feet, for convenience. Gravity at the surface of the Earth, thirty-two feet per second per second. The square root of twenty million over thirty-two would be two hundred and fifty times the square root of ten ... times *pi* ... about twenty-five hundred seconds. Call it forty-two minutes. He ran through the calculation once more, found no error.

Very well, in forty-two minutes, if he was right, he would be emerging from the far side of the planet. In the meantime, the rotation of the Earth would have brought his exit point about ten or eleven degrees westward. ... It was all right: that would still be in the ocean.

He took a deep breath. At least he would come *out*, not cycle inside the Earth until his momentum was used up. If his calculations were right—

How long had he been falling?

Cursing himself, he fumbled for his wristwatch. The dial was not luminous, but with a nail-file from his pocket he pried up the crystal, felt the hands with his fingertips. They indicated about ten minutes after nine. He had been falling for what seemed half an hour or more, but was probably less than five minutes. Assume, then, that he had begun his fall at 9.05 by this watch. The time it showed was local California time as of 1980 A.D. – curious to think of this mechanism still faithfully keeping track of the minutes now buried thousand of years in the past ... but that did not matter.

At 9.47, he should emerge. If friction was a negligible factor, and he could not assume otherwise, then he would rise to a height of two or three hundred feet above the ocean ... too high. He felt himself begin to sweat, as he realized that it would be necessary to chance falling back through the Earth – all the way through to the Western hemisphere, then back again, hoping that in those two additional passages, friction would bring him out at a level from which he could hope to fall safely.

Luckily, there was plenty of room in the ocean. Two more passages would bring him westward only twenty-odd degrees. ...

A feeling of discomfort drew his attention. He was uneasy: what had he been neglecting?

Friction: what if it were *not* negligible? For that matter, what about the interior heat of the Earth?

He was to pass near the center of the core, which was thought to be at about four *thousand* degrees centigrade ...

Something was wrong. He reached out quickly, touched the hollow curve of the force-shell. It was neither warm nor cool to his senses. But he had already been falling ... he felt the hands of the watch again ... more than six minutes ... *t* squared, call it a hundred thirty thousand, times one-half the acceleration – two million feet, or something close to *four hundred miles.*

While part of his mind tried to grasp that, another part went on coldly calculating.

Temperature of the Earth's crust increased with depth, by about thirty degrees centigrade every kilometer. And the shell he was in was transparent to visible light. Therefore ...

He was through the crust, falling through the mantle.

He should have passed the red-heat stage long ago; by now he should be well into the white. And yet—

He touched the shell again. It was still neither hot nor cold. The darkness was unbroken.

Doubt struck him. Was he really falling? Suppose he was simply hanging here, suspended, without gravity ... drifting like a disembodied spirit, forever under the Earth?

He gripped the crossbar fiercely. The Universe obeyed certain laws, among these were the mutual attraction of material bodies and the equivalence of gravity and inertia. His senses told him that he was falling, and in this case it happened to be true – he *was* falling.

He touched the hands of the watch once more. They seemed hardly to have moved. He held the watch to his ear to listen for the whirr of the motor, then swore at himself impatiently. Of course the watch was running: it was his own perception of time that was at fault.

If he only had a light ... He would be seeing what no man had ever seen, the rocks of the deep mantle. In a few minutes he would be passing through the rim of the outer core, into that curious region where nickel-iron was compressed into a liquid....

The watch again. The minute hand had moved, just perceptibly. Falling into this dark emptiness. Naismith could not help thinking again of lost spirits, wandering forever under the Earth. The Greeks had imagined a Hell like that; the Egyptians, too. A phrase from some chance reading came back to him: 'the chthonic ourobouros.'

He shuddered, and gripped the crossbar hard. *I am a man, not a ghost.*

He wondered if what he was experiencing had ever happened before: if any other living soul had made this incredible plunge. Such a man, failing to reach the surface again, swinging back and forth, thousands of times ... until eventually his lifeless body came to rest at the center of the Earth.

What would have happened then, when the machine's power ran out? A gigantic explosion, probably violent enough to cause vulcanism all over the planet, perhaps even shift the balance of the continents. ... Therefore it had probably never happened.

But suppose the power had *never* run out? Then what was left of the man must be still hanging there ... or perhaps a cluster of corpses, each in his shell of force ...

Time passed. In the darkness and silence, Naismith found himself becoming intensely aware of his physical substance – his body's attitude, the partly flexed limbs, the sense of half-perceived processes going on inside him. What a curious and almost incredible thing it was, after all, to be a living man!

For four years he had believed himself to be Gordon Naismith. Then he had been told that this identity was a mask, that in reality he was a member of a different race, from a world twenty thousand years in the future. ... But this identity was no more real to him than the other.

What was the truth? Where had he really come from, and what was the goal to which he felt himself so irresistibly driven?

Blurred, illusory shapes swam before his eyes in the darkness. He blinked irritably, then closed his eyes, but the shapes remained. He felt himself growing drowsy.

He came awake with a start, realizing that time had passed. He felt the hands of the watch. It was nine-thirty. Twenty-five minutes had gone by. But—

Naismith clutched the crossbar hard, as the icy shock struck him. In twenty-two minutes, he should have reached the center of the Earth. Surely, at that depth, there would have been some rise in temperature in the capsule!

He reached out, touched the shell. It was just perceptibly warm.

He deliberately let five minutes go by, then touched the shell again. It was definitely warmer....

Was there a delay factor in the capsule's transmission of heat? Or had he somehow taken longer than twenty-two minutes to reach the center? But that was impossible.

Again he waited five minutes before he touched the shell. This time there was no mistake: it was hot.

After a moment, even the air in the capsule began to seem unpleasantly warm and heavy. Naismith found he was sweating; his clothes began to stick to him.

After five minutes more, it was not necessary to touch the wall again. It was glowing dull red.

Two minutes dragged by. The shell brightened through the red, into the orange, yellow, then white.

Naismith was in agony. Even with his eyes tight shut, the glare and heat were unendurable. He was being burnt alive.

He buried his face in his arms, sobbing for breath. The heat pressed in relentlessly upon him from all sides; he could feel it like a heavy weight on his clothing. Now he could smell his hair beginning to crisp and smolder.

The metal framework grew too hot to touch. Naismith retreated from it as far as he could, touching it only with the soles of his feet; but to do so was to draw nearer to the white-hot shell of the capsule.

He groaned aloud.

It seemed to him, after a moment, that the heat and glare

had abated a little. He opened his eyes warily. It was true: the shell had turned from white to orange. As he watched, it faded slowly into the red.

Naismith breathed in a great, tortured gasp of relief. The crisis was over – he was going to live!

Time – he must notice the time. Ignoring the pain of his blistered skin, he felt for the hands of the watch. It was exactly ten o'clock.

His passage through Inferno had taken about fifteen minutes.

Ten o'clock – fifty-five minutes from the beginning of his fall. By now, if his calculations had been correct, he should have emerged on the far side of the planet.

But he had just passed through a zone of heat that could only be the core!

The air in the capsule was growing cooler by the moment. The shell faded from dull red into hot darkness again. A few minutes later, Naismith dared to touch it cautiously; it was hot, but bearable.

Naismith felt totally bewildered. The period of his transit through the Earth *had* to be approximately forty-two minutes, no matter from what height he began his fall. Could his watch be running too slowly? Was time in the capsule moving at a rate different from that of time outside?

As the fall continued in darkness, Naismith grew aware of both hunger and thirst. He had been penned up here for only about an hour, and that ought to be well within his tolerance; but how long was this going on? How long could he last?

Once more, by an effort of will, he calmed his mind. The shell steadily cooled; otherwise no change was perceptible.

If he assumed a lag in the capsule's absorption and reradiation of heat, Naismith drowsily thought, then it could be supposed that he had reached the mid-point of his orbit in just about twice the predicted time. That would imply that there *was* a difference of time-rate inside the capsule, or else that some other factor had been reduced for unknown reasons....

For a moment he allowed himself to speculate on what he would do to the two aliens, if by some incredible chance he came out of this alive and met them again; but he cut off the thought. He felt himself drifting again into sleep, and abandoned himself to it willingly.

He snapped back to awareness with a start. How long had he been dozing?

He felt the watch. It was 10.17. He had been in free fall for seventy-two minutes.

Tension began to build in him again. Unless his understanding of the situation was simply, grossly wrong, then the zone of heat he had passed *must* have been the core of the Earth; and his period must be about twice what he had originally calculated. But why?

Time dragged. It was 10.19; then 10.23; then 10.27. Naismith waited tensely. Ten-nineteen. Now, if ever—

One moment he was still in utter blackness. The next, stars bloomed out beneath him, a galaxy of them, blindingly brilliant in their half-globe of night. Above him was a dark orb that occluded the other half of the sky; it was drifting away as he watched.

Naismith blinked up at it in uncomprehending wonder for a moment, until he realized that it was the night side of the Earth – that he had burst out of it feet-foremost.

His breath caught, and tears came to his eyes. He was *out*, out in the free air at last! He made an instinctive attempt to squirm around right-side-to, but gave it up immediately; that did not matter.

What did matter, he realized with sudden alarm, was that he was rising too high! The wrinkled, starlit face of the water was drawing away overhead – five hundred feet, a thousand, with no sign of slowing down.

The time had been too long; his speed was too great.

Coming down, Naismith realized with horror, he would be going much too fast to dare turn off the machine ...

He would have to go all the way through, past that inferno of heat – at least once, perhaps twice. He was grimly sure that he could not survive even one more passage.

The globe above him continued to recede. Now it was concave, a gigantic silver-lit bowl: now it turned convex. The sky beneath changed from blue-black to purple, to ebony. The stars shone with a crueler sharpness.

Veils of cloud whisked by and receded, dwindling. How was it possible that he should be rising so far? He must be nearly into the stratosphere.

Now his speed was diminishing. He hung fixed in space for an instant, then saw the Earth creeping nearer again.

On the whole broad, overhanging curve of the ocean, there was not one light, not a ship. His ascent had taken perhaps a minute and a half; in the same length of time he must plunge back into the sea.

Naismith stared at the immense globe as it swelled toward him. There must be some explanation! It was out of the question for a falling body to come up ten or fifteen miles higher than the point it had started from ... Unless—

Suddenly Naismith remembered the instant of his fall, and the seeming nightmare slowness of it, while he fought to escape the shell of the force-field he was in.

Make this assumption: that the relation of the machine to the normal physical universe was such that its gravitational interactions were reduced ... that it fell, say, with half or a quarter the normal velocity.

He ran through the calculations quickly, with growing excitement. Substituting one-quarter *g* gave him a figure of eighty-five minutes, which was almost exactly right.

There was an apparent violation here either of the conservation of energy or the principle of equivalence, but never mind that now ... The consequence was that during his fall, he would tend to swing out away from the Sun, being less attracted to that body than the Earth was. The center of his orbit would be displaced a few miles, just enough to account for this rise....

The globe of the Earth was rushing toward him. Naismith watched it grimly, thinking that the next time he approached the surface it would be somewhere in the Pacific, about forty-two degrees west of Lake Michigan. Then eighty-four minutes back again; this time he would come out somewhere near the 63rd meridian, still in the Indian Ocean.

Now the dark surface was hurtling down at express-train speed. Naismith involuntarily braced himself, even though he knew there would be no sense of contact. He saw a whorl of bluish light just above him, expanding, rushing down. His eyes widened; he had just time to gasp, then something struck him a murderous blow.

The universe wheeled majestically around him; there was pain deep in his head. The stars slowly darkened and went out.

12

He was aware of having been unconscious, of a pain in his head, and of a wordless anxiety that had driven him up out of sleep.

He opened his eyes.

He was looking up into a gulf of blue sky, dotted with clouds. Hardness pressed against his back; the air he breathed was cool and pure. Something dry and flexible brushed his cheek as he turned his head; vague yellowish rod-shapes moved across his vision. He sucked in a breath, rolled over and sat up.

He was on the ground, with grass shoulder-high all around him. A few feet away, on the trampled grass, lay a small blued-steel machine.

Naismith stared at it in frozen surprise for an instant, before he realized it was not the same one the aliens had used: the shape was similar, but not identical.

He reached for it, and found himself held back, although he could neither see nor feel any obstacle. Incredulous, he put out his full strength, straining until the blood roared in his ears; but he could not force his body an inch closer to the machine.

After a moment he gave it up, and cautiously got to his feet. He felt no restraint, and was able to stand; but when he tried to take a step toward the machine, the same impalpable barrier held him back.

He straightened again, looking out over the sea of grass. At first he saw only the rolling yellow waves, with an occasional green treetop in the distance, and a line of misty hills along the horizon. Then he became aware of movement.

A few hundred yards away across the plain, a human form was moving slowly through the grass. It was a girl, the upper part of her body either nude or lightly clothed; her legs and hips were hidden by the grass. She was walking with leisurely grace, halting occasionally, with her face turned up to the sun. He could not make out her features, but something in the lines and the motion of her body made him think she was young.

She had not noticed him. Naismith glanced again at the machine on the ground, then crouched out of sight and once more began a desperate effort to approach it. He found that he could walk in a circle around the machine, but could never come any nearer. He dug his feet in and pushed, with some idea of forcing the machine to move ahead of him, but did not succeed.

He stopped, gasping for breath, and looked over the tops of the grasses again. The girl was much closer. This time she saw him.

Naismith stood up and waited.

The girl walked unhurriedly toward him. Her skin was tanned, her hair coppery, shining in the light. She was dressed, or half dressed, in bits of contoured metal and fabric that clung to her body here and there, in a pattern more esthetic than functional. Her eyes were narrowed as she walked, as if she were aware of nothing but the caress of sun and air on her body.

She waited until she was only a few yards away before

she spoke. 'Awake already?' she said. The language she used was BoDen.

Naismith did not reply. Seen so near at hand, the girl had a startling, provocative beauty. Her skin was satiny, as if covered by an almost invisible sheer tissue – spiderweb-stuff that ended, without a visible border, at the edges of her lips and eyes. The red-violet of her lips might have been natural or artificial. Her eyes were pale green, fringed with dark lashes, startling against her brown face.

She was watching him with an amused expression. 'Well, don't stand there – back away.'

Naismith did not move. 'Who are you – what is this place?'

'Earth, of course. Now back off so that I can get in.'

Naismith glanced down at the machine, then back at the girl. 'What if I don't?'

'I'll leave you here until you get hungry.'

Naismith shrugged, backed off a few steps into the tall grass. The girl waited, then darted forward to the machine. She sat down on the ground beside it, folding her legs neatly, and looked up at him with a mocking smile. 'All right, you can come back.'

Naismith looked at her, then stared around at the grassy plain, peaceful and silent under the sky.

Absently he let his fingers trail through the dry, bearded grasses.

Far off, the tiny dot of a bird launched itself from one of the isolated treetops; he followed it across the sky until it alighted again.

'This is a beautiful spot,' he said.

Her laughter made him turn. 'Like to see what it's really like?' she said. She tossed something toward him. 'Here.'

Naismith's hand went up automatically to bat the thing away; at the last moment he changed his mind, plucked it out of the air.

It was a shaped blue grip of some smooth, waxy substance. When his hand closed around it, a disk of dark color glowed into being just above it.

He stared at the thing in perplexity for a moment before he realized that he was looking *through* the disk, at a three-dimensional scene beyond. He turned the grip this way and that, swung it around, and discovered that the view through the disk corresponded with the landscape around him – horizon, hills, the plain itself were all there, but all changed.

Grass and trees were gone; instead, there was raw earth and rock – blackened, cratered and barren under a starred purple sky. The sun blazed overhead – not the ordinary ball of light, but a monstrous thing with flames spreading high from either side. Naismith lowered the disk, puzzled.

'What is that – another time line?' he asked.

'I told you,' she said looking up at him serenely. 'That is what is really here. Everything you see is only a clever illusion.' She indicated the landscapc around them. 'Earth is a dead planet now – destroyed by wars. You could not even breathe here, if you were not protected by this machine.'

Naismith frowned, and put out a hand to touch the nearest clump of grass. The dry stems, the bearded tips, were real to his fingers. He pulled up a few, wadded them in his palm, watched them fall.

'I don't believe you,' he said flatly. 'Who would do such a thing?'

'They say Zugs did it,' she answered indifferently. 'The proof is that only human beings see any of this – a camera will not photograph it, and the illusion will not pass through that viewer. Give it back.'

After a moment's hesitation, Naismith tossed the grip to her. The disk winked out as it left his hand, winked on again as she caught it. She glanced through it, said with a trace of bitterness, 'All dust and stone,' and put it away in her silver belt.

'Then why were you walking out there?' Naismith asked curiously.

She shrugged her bare shoulders. 'It's beautiful,' she said. 'Why shouldn't I enjoy it, just because it's an illusion?' She gazed up at him. 'Well, get in.'

Naismith stepped closer, watching as she picked up the

machine. 'Where are you taking me?'

Without replying, she touched the controls of the machine. A faint jolt came, and they were enclosed in a transparent bubble, through which the landscape shone spectral blue. Almost at once, without any feeling of motion, the earth droppd away underneath, the sky began to darken.

Naismith leaned forward slightly, found that the same barrier kept him from approaching the girl. She smiled up at him mockingly, and lit a green cigarette with jeweled fingers that trembled slightly. 'Sit down, Shefth.'

Naismith obeyed slowly, staring at her. 'I remember now,' he said. 'I saw something blue coming up, then—'

She nodded, blowing a jet of greenish smoke. 'I didn't dare take a chance with you,' she said. 'I hit you with a force-rod as I pulled you in. Then I thought I might as well wait till you woke up, so I went forward a few thousand years and landed down there.' She moistened her lips. 'You're strong,' she said. 'By all the rules, you should have been unconscious for at least another twenty minutes. Anyhow, I had time to put a mind helmet on you and read all your little secrets.'

Naismith felt his body tensing. 'What secrets?'

'I know them *all*,' she said, wagging her head wisely. 'All about California, and the two Uglies you called Lall and Churan.' She laughed. 'And what they wanted you to do.'

Naismith stared at her, eyes narrowed. 'Do you speak English?' he asked abruptly.

She did not respond.

'Do you know that you are a dirty little slut?' he asked in the same even tone.

Her eyes blazed at him. Her lips pulled away from her teeth, and for an instant Naismith felt a chill of alarm. Then it was gone.

'I won't kill you now,' she whispered in English. 'That would be too easy. When I kill you, it will be slowly and painfully, to teach you not to speak that way to Liss-Yani.'

Naismith caught his breath, then pointed a finger at her. 'Now I know you,' he said. 'It was your voice, that night, when I saw the Zug. You said "Kill it" in just the same tone. You sent that – vision, whatever it was. And those dreams— Why?'

She blinked at him. 'Aren't you afraid?'

'Why should I be? You said you're not going to kill me now.'

'And later?'

'Later, maybe I'll be afraid.'

'I wonder,' she said, licking her moist violet lips. She stubbed the cigarette abruptly into a hole in the floor, and it vanished. 'What's your name?' she asked.

'Gordon Naismith.'

'Not that. Your real name, what is it?'

'I don't remember,' said Naismith.

She looked at him thoughtfully. 'And you don't remember anything about the City, or the death collars, or Thera-Yani?'

'No.'

She sighed. 'I wish I could believe you. Come here and kiss me.' She tilted up her face and sat waiting, hands on the control box.

After a surprised instant, Naismith slid toward her. The invisible barrier halted him, then seemed to soften; it melted away until his face approached hers; but when he tried to extend his arms, they were stopped in mid-air.

'Well, come on,' she said, half-closing her eyes.

Naismith, half annoyed, half intrigued, leaned forward and kissed her. Her lips were soft, hot and moist; they parted under his at once, and her soft tongue probed into his mouth.

After a few moments, she lay back and pushed him away. 'Is that your best effort?' she asked. 'Go on, sit down.' She plucked another green cigarette out of the floor and lit it. 'Well, I never heard of a Shefth that could kiss.'

Nettled, he asked, 'Then why did you suggest it?'

'I wanted to see what you would do. A real Shefth would not kiss a Yani.' She cocked her head at him. 'Actually, it was not *too* bad.'

Naismith stared at her in surprise for a moment, then

laughed. Remembering the world of his dreams, he thought, No, of course a Shefth would not kiss a Yani; and she had all the stigmata – the coppery skin and hair, green eyes, slender, tapering fingers....

'How did you know where to find me?' he asked in Bo-Den. 'Were you watching, all that time I was with Lall and Churan?'

'Of course. Uglies are very stupid. They thought you would simply drop into the Earth and never come out again. But I knew better. I computed your orbit, and—' She shrugged. 'Then it was easy.'

Her fingers were slowly stroking one of the buttons on the control box she held on the floor. Naismith said, 'You know, of course, that it was on your account the Uglies decided they couldn't trust me?'

'I know.'

'Then why can't *you* trust me?' he demanded. 'Either I'm on one side or the other.'

'Because there's something wrong about you,' she said, and blew green smoke at him. 'I felt it when I kissed you, and I am never mistaken. I don't know what it is – you seem to be just what you say, a Shefth who has lost his memory. But there is ... something. Oh, well – forget it.' She touched the control box, then leaned back against the wall. 'Are you hungry? Thirsty?'

At once Naismith was again acutely aware of both needs. Watching him, the girl reached behind her to the wall, withdrew a cup of foaming white liquid and a brownish, solid cake. She broke the cake in half, offered him the cup and one piece of the brownish stuff.

Naismith accepted both, but cautiously watched the girl nibble at the cake before he tried it himself. It was chewy and rich-tasting, something like figs. He sipped the liquid, found it agreeably astringent.

The girl laughed suddenly.

'What is it?' Naismith demanded, lowering the cup.

'You were so easy,' she said. 'How did you know I did not put ten-day poison in the fruit or wine?'

Naismith stared at her. 'Did you?'

'Maybe.' Her eyes glittered with amusement. 'If I did, you can only get the antidote from me. So if I ask you a favor, later on, you *may* want to do it instead of taking a chance.'

'What sort of a favor?' Naismith asked. He glanced at the food, laid it down.

'Go on, eat! If there *is* poison in it, you've had enough already – the rest won't make any difference.'

Naismith looked at her grimly, then nodded and took another bite of the cake. 'What sort of a favor?' he repeated.

'I don't know,' she said indifferently. 'Things were becoming a little difficult when I left. The Barrier is so close now. It doesn't hurt to have friends at a time like that.'

In spite of himself, Naismith smiled. 'Is that your idea of a friend – someone who has to do what you say because you've poisoned him?'

'Please don't be dull,' she said, with a *moue* of distaste. 'After all, we are going to be in this traveler together for another ten minutes.'

'Then what happens?'

'I hand you over to the Circle,' she said without interest. She thrust out one hand, looking complacently at the nacrous violet of her nails. 'Do you like this color?'

'It's very pretty. The Circle – what do they want from me?'

'They think you can kill the Zug. They are terribly worried about it.'

'Then that part was true?'

'About the Zug? Oh, yes. This is total-access clothing, did you know that?' She touched the curved and ornamented plaques that clung to her body one after another. Each one winked briefly out of existence, revealing an arm, a breast with a rather startling violet nipple, a hip, a thigh.

Naismith felt an intense, momentary interest in that tender-looking flesh, but he put it aside. 'Which faction is ascendant in the Circle now?' he demanded.

The girl frowned. 'What a dull thing you are! You Shefti, actually ...' She yawned once more and stretched back against the curved blue-mist wall. 'I think I shall take a little rest.' Her eyes closed.

Naismith gazed at her in annoyance, but before he could speak, something new in the sky caught his attention. It was a mass of spectral blue globes, hanging motionless at eye level: it had not been there a moment ago.

'What *is* that?' Naismith demanded.

The girl opened her eyes briefly. 'The City,' she said.

At first her words seemed irrelevant. Then a shock went through Naismith's body. 'Do you mean *that* is the City?' he demanded.

She sat up, eyes wide open. 'What's wrong with you?'

Naismith did not reply. His pseudo-memories of the City were all of gigantic rooms, corridors, floating shapes, crowds of people.

Now that he looked for it, the knowledge was there: but it had never once occurred to him that the City was not on Earth.

His inner agitation increased. *Here* was the danger, not in Liss-Yani's petulant threats.

His knowledge of essential things was incomplete, badly organized, not readily available. What other blunders might he not make at some crucial moment? ... And how much longer did he have to prepare himself?

Outside, the huge, complex shape ponderously revolved as they drew nearer. A bull's-eye pattern rolled into view, centered itself in the mass, grew steadily larger. The inner circle yawned and swallowed them. They were inside.

13

Through the walls of the time vehicle, Naismith found himself looking into a huge globular room – a hollow, pale-green sphere, with regular markings at intervals on its surface, in which floated a confusing array of objects.

Liss-Yani smiled at him sidelong, her hand on the control box. 'Are you ready?'

He stared back at her, said nothing.

Smiling, she did something to the controls. The time vehicle winked out of being.

At the same instant, something dark and incredibly swift flapped toward them, enclosing them. Naismith flung up his arms in instinctive defense, then relaxed. Somewhere a bell was ringing.

'What is this?'

'A precaution,' she said, enjoying his reaction. 'What if we had been Uglies?'

Through the dark transparency around them, Naismith could dimly perceive motion in the great globe. Angular machines drifted nearer, lenses glowing sullen red, like coals in the heart of a fire. A little above them, another shape was moving: Naismith realized suddenly that it was a man. Something was wrong with the legs, but he could make out pipestem arms, a head, the glint of eyes staring.

Abruptly the bell stopped; the darkness winked out. They were floating in the middle of the green sphere, surrounded by machines in whose lenses the red glow was dying. Nearer, the man Naismith had seen before was floating toward them, body at an angle to theirs, hands gripping his forearms, like a Mandarin. He was dressed in a fantastic, puffed and ruffled garment of yellow and white stripes, the top a short-sleeved singlet, the lower part of a tube covering both legs and closed at the bottom with a yellow bow. His face was lean and gnomish, at once anguished and ironic. His eyes glittered; his wide mouth twitched. 'You got him, I see,' he said.

'Yes, here he is, Prell.'

'Is he dangerous?'

The girl turned slowly in mid-air and gazed at Naismith. 'I'm not sure,' she said thoughtfully.

'We'd better keep the automatics on him, for the time being. Later they'll give him a collar.' Prell turned in the air, spoke a single, harsh word.

Out of the clutter of objects hanging in the vast space, one drifted nearer: it was a miniature white sarcophagus, with a design painted on it in blue and yellow. The drawing was a crude sketch of a young girl with yellow hair, eyes closed, lips demurely smiling. Her hands were crossed over her breast.

'Tell the Highborn,' said Prell, 'the attempt was successful. We have the Shefth.'

The sarcophagus clicked, hummed, drifted away again.

'Probably it will take a while to get her attention,' said Prell. 'Do you want to look at the work, in the meantime?'

'Yes, all right,' said the girl indifferently. The two of them turned, drifted rapidly away from Naismith. After a moment, already tiny in the distance, they paused and looked back, with comical expressions of surprise on their faces.

'I forgot,' said Prell's distant voice; 'he doesn't have a director. Wait a moment.' He spoke the harsh word again; another machine drifted toward him. This one was box-shaped, ornamented with red and green arabesques on a black ground. 'A director for that man,' said Prell, pointing.

The box dipped slightly, turned, and came rocketing down at Naismith. At the last moment it slowed, came to a halt facing him a yard away.

'For my information, sir,' said a musical voice from the box, 'what is that man's name?'

'Naismith,' said Naismith, looking at it curiously.

'Excuse me, sir, but that is not a catalogued name,' said the box politely.

The voices of Prell and the girl murmured together a moment; then Prell said, 'We'll get him a name presently. For now, just call him "that man".'

'Thank you, sir,' said the box. A hopper in its center slowly opened; out floated a narrow, flexible band of some cream-colored substance.

'Put it on your wrist,' called the girl. Naismith did so, and the stuff curled around his wrist as if half-alive, clung to itself and seemed to melt together; the seam disappeared.

'Now point in the direction you want to go and just tense your wrist slightly,' her voice went on.

Naismith did as he was told, and found the vast green sphere rotating slowly around him, while certain distant clumps of machines drifted nearer. When Prell and the girl came into view again, he pointed toward them, and this time managed to keep them centered. He lowered his arm, came to rest a few feet away.

'You'll get used to it,' said Liss-Yani. 'Come on!'

She and Prell moved off again, but came to a halt almost immediately. Naismith jockeyed up beside them. Prell was moving some small glittering objects across the vacant air before him: suddenly there was a shimmer, a crackle, and a great round sheet of silvery reflection came into being.

Prell touched it again; the disk turned transparent, and they were looking into another room, darker and even more enormous than the one they were in. In the vast space myriads of tiny shapes were moving: some were human, some were symmetrical forms of machines – boxes, sarcophagi, vase shapes. As Naismith's vision adjusted to the scene, he began to make out serried ranks of dark objects, not visibly connected to another, among which the human and robot forms came and went.

Prell reached out again, and the scene appeared to drift nearer. They were looking down upon one of the thousands of ranked machines, over which a gnomish young man in a dress like Prell's was hovering.

'This is the Barrier control network,' the girl's voice explained. 'They've been working on it for five years. It's almost finished.'

'Is this an actual entranceway into that room,' Naismith asked, fumbling for words, 'or a – a viewscreen?'

Prell looked at him curiously. 'What is the difference?'

Naismith realized, in confusion, that there was no difference, in the question as he had asked it: the two phrases, in BoDen, were almost identical.

While he was still thinking dazedly of the implications of this, Prell reached out again.

'Would you like to see what they're doing?' he asked. Without waiting for a reply, he gestured once more with the shining object in his hand.

Part of the scene before them seemed to expand. Where one of the floating machines had been, there was a dim lattice of crystals, growing more shadowy and insubstantial as it swelled; then darkness, then a dazzle of faint prismatic light – tiny complexes in a vast three-dimensional array, growing steadily bigger...

Naismith caught his breath. He realized that he was seeing the very molecules that made up the substance of the machines that were being built in the next chamber.

'This is why it takes so long,' Prell said, rubbing his forearms nervously. He grimaced. 'Every channel has to be built up molecule by molecule, under rigid control. Like to see it closer?'

The magnification increased. In luminous darkness, Naismith saw molecules scattered like tiny planets. A moving dot of light appeared, slowly traced a mathematical arc across the blackness. Other arcs of light sprang out from it, like ribs from a spinal column; slowly, the dots that were molecules drifted across to take position upon them.

'Is that direct vision, or a display of some kind?' Naismith demanded, fascinated.

'It's a mathematical analogue,' Prell answered. 'Just a toy, really.' His mouth twitched; he scrubbed at his wrists as if in pain.

'It's beautiful,' said Naismith.

Prell shot him a startled glance, then seemed to go into a reverie.

The sarcophagus robot drifted up, said discreetly, 'The Highborn has received your message. She asks you to send that man to the social room.'

'All right,' said Prell. 'Liss-Yani, you might as well take him over. Come back later, I want to talk to you.'

'Yes,' she said. Turning, she took Naismith's arm. 'This way.'

Naismith's body was trembling in alarm. The thought came: *Prell is dangerous. He knows what I am.*

Brain working furiously, he allowed the girl to lead him away from Prell. *His reactions are slow – he is still thinking about it. But in another few seconds ...*

The girl came to a halt in mid-air; awkwardly, Naismith stabilized himself beside her. Before them, faintly, he could make out a silvery circle in the air. Liss-Yani reached out, touched it with a glittering object, as Prell had done before. The ten-foot circle quivered, rippled: they were looking into a gigantic room full of color and motion. 'Come,' said the girl again, pulling him through.

On the opposite side, Naismith brought himself to a halt, looking back. He could still see the scientist, hovering in thought beside one of his machines. The girl's arm reached past him, touched the circle, and the scene blanked out, was gone.

Naismith whirled. 'Teach me how to operate these doorways,' he said angrily.

'It's perfectly easy,' she said, staring at him. 'You just touch them with the opener and think about where you want to go. There'll be plenty of time for that – come on.'

'Give it to me,' he said, holding out his hand. After a moment she shrugged, put a smooth silvery object into his palm. It felt like plastic rather than metal; it was an elongated ovoid, fitting naturally into his hand so that the blunt tip of it projected.

Naismith reached out, touched the circle. The view sprang

into being again. Prell had turned slightly, was massaging his forearms with his hands; there was an anxious expression on his face.

'One moment,' said Naismith. He propelled himself through the opening, turned, touched it with the silvery object again; it blanked out. Instantly Naismith hurled himself at Prell.

The scientist turned, with a startled expression, as Naismith hurtled up. Naismith seized the man by the front of his robe, yanked Prell toward him. Terror sprang into the little man's eyes.

'What was my mistake?' Naismith demanded. 'Tell me!' He tightened his grip.

'Beautiful,' the little man gasped. His mouth opened and closed like a fish's, making no sound, until Naismith impatiently shook him. 'You're not – a Shefth ... They have no – esthetic responses ...' His face contorted with sudden malevolence. 'I know what you are – help!—' His lungs filled, he opened his mouth to shout.

Naismith gripped his frail body with one arm, put the other forearm against his chin, pressed. There was a gurgling sound as the man's wind was cut off; then a dry, loud snap. The body sagged.

As Naismith turned, one of the ubiquitous machines drifted nearer. 'For my information, sir,' it said musically, 'what has happened to Master Prell?'

'Uglies attacked him,' said Naismith at random, moving away. 'They appeared suddenly, killed Prell, then vanished.'

'The automatic weapons did not fire,' said the machine politely.

'They were out of order,' Naismith said. He glanced around; none of the other floating robots seemed to have noticed anything. Could he disable this one, if he had to? Was it necessary?

'For my information, sir,' said the robot, 'which were out of order, the automatic weapons or the Uglies?'

'The weapons,' Naismith told it, staring at the intricate design on the front of the box.

'Thank you, sir.'

'For my information,' Naismith said suddenly, 'tell me, are you intelligent?'

'I am intelligent. I have a machine intelligence of plus forty.'

Naismith frowned. 'That was not what I wanted to know. Are you – are you conscious?'

'I am not conscious, sir.'

'Have you volition?'

'I have no volition, sir.'

'Thank you.'

'Thank you, sir.' The machine dipped politely, turned, drifted away.

On the other side of the doorway, the girl was waiting. Naismith slipped through, closed the circle quickly behind him.

'What took you so long?' she demanded.

'I had trouble finding the doorway again,' he said. Breathing hard, he stared around at the crowded immensity behind her. The room was globular, and so vast that he could not estimate its extent. In a pale greenish haze, what seemed to be thousands of floating bodies were ranked: some coming and going, in a slow circling movement, others fixed. In a given group, large or small, all the heads would be pointing one way and the bodies spaced about equally, like fish in a school. Some were right-side up from his point of view, others upside down, others at all angles. It gave him a vertiginous feeling.

'Well, come on,' said the girl.

Naismith hesitated. Things were moving too fast; he needed time to think. It was incredible that he had just committed a murder ... This was not like the other time, when he had blanked out and discovered later that he had killed Wells. This time, something in his own brain had said, *Prell knows what I am.* For the moment, he had known exactly what he had to do and why. Now it was fading. ... *In God's name,* he thought suddenly, *what kind of a monster am I?*

14

He was aware that the girl had taken his hand, was tugging him off toward the center of the sphere. After a moment Naismith cooperated, using his own director. They passed a little shoal of brightly dressed people, then another. The room was full of the tiny sarcophagus-shaped robots, too, Naismith noticed. Then, with a shock, he realized that many of the floating bodies were those of greenskinned Uglies.

They were carrying things, moving this way and that on errands, their faces expressionless. Some of the brightly dressed people were self-propelled, like himself and Liss-Yani; but others were being moved from one place to another by Uglies or by robots. All of them wore garments like Prell's that seemed to hide stunted or atrophied legs.

Naismith and the girl rounded a huge, complex spray-shape of glittering golden material, through the branches of which tiny fish-shaped robots swam. On the further side, past a throng of floating people, Naismith caught sight of another huge object, this one as hideous as the other was beautiful.

It was the torso of a female Ugly, magnified to the size of a ten-story building. Gigantic and grotesque, it loomed over the glittering throng like a human body surrounded by may-flies. Its arms were secured behind its back; its skin was pierced here and there by long needles, from which drops of dark blood were slowly oozing. Through the echoing talk and laughter, Naismith suddenly heard a hoarse bawling sound – a groan, immensely amplified, that seemed to come from where the Ugly's head should be. The talk died away for a moment, then there was a scattering of laughter, and the hum of conversation began again.

Naismith felt sickened. 'What's that?' he demanded.

'A solid,' the girl answered indifferently. 'That's one of the rebel Uglies they captured. They made a big solid of her so everyone can watch. Look over there.'

Naismith turned his head, saw a girl of Liss-Yani's caste entwined in a sexual embrace with a slender, muscular man. There was a little ring of spectators around them, and some languid applause.

'No, not them,' the girl said impatiently. 'Look farther up.'

Naismith did so, and saw nothing of interest except still another woman of the Entertainer class – dressed, this one, in long gossamer robes – drifting across the room with an entourage of young men and women. Her face was noble and sad; she looked straight ahead, without expression.

'That's Thera-Yani,' said the girl in a muted voice. 'Isn't she wonderful!'

'I don't see it,' Naismith said. 'Why wonderful?'

'She was the best-loved Yani in the City until last month, when the new mutations were released and the fashion changed. Now there is nothing left for her. She took twenty-day poison, and she is saying her farewells to the City.'

Naismith snorted, unimpressed. Up ahead, a greenskinned female servant was pushing a tremendously fat old woman across the air by the small of her back. The Ugly, Naismith noticed, was wearing a bright metal collar around her neck; he now recalled seeing similar collars on other greenskins.

A fragment of speech drifted back: 'But why must *all* the Uglies die, Mistress? Haven't I always been good, haven't I always—'

'Oh, don't be tiresome, Menda. I explained to you before, I can't do anything about it. It's something to do with *science*. Don't let me hear ...'

Now they were approaching the center of the enormous room, where the largest and most tightly packed mass of people floated. The shrill hum of conversation grew louder. Naismith's nerves prickled; the closeness of all these people was subtly unpleasant.

Up ahead, a raucous female voice was screaming, like an articulate parrot's: the words were not distinguishable. Naismith and the girl moved nearer, threading their way patiently through the press, sometimes horizontally, sometimes in the vertical plane.

At last Naismith could make out the screaming woman. She hung in the middle of a little group of gaudily dressed people. She was hugely, obscenely fat in her puffed and ornamented garment of white and scarlet. When she swung around, Naismith could see her body quake like a jelly inside the fabric. Her face was sallow and lined, the eyes bright with madness. '... come in here and tell me, who do you think you are, be silent and listen. I tell you I will not have such disrespect, why don't you observe the rules, don't talk back to me, I tell you, listen ...'

'Highborn, if you please,' said a fat man in brown, with ruffles around his worried baby-pink face.

'... never in three hundred years have I been treated like this, be quiet, Truglen, I wasn't speaking to you, how can I bear these constant interruptions, Regg! Regg! where is the creature, Regg!'

'Yes, Highborn,' said a greenskinned man, floating up beside her.

'Give me a pickup, can't you see the state I'm in?'

'Highborn,' said another man, almost as fat as the first, 'try to be calm. You may want to wait a little before you have another of those, recall that you've already had ten this period ...'

'Don't tell me how many I've had, how dare you?' She choked apoplectically, took something the greenskin was holding out, swallowed it and glared, speechless for a moment. The servant handed her a tube leading to a flask of reddish fluid, and she sucked at it, her old face hollowing deeply and her mad eyes bulging.

Liss-Yani spoke to a robot, which glided forward and said politely, 'Highborn, here is the Shefth you sent for.'

Her head swiveled; she glared, spat out the drinking tube. 'And high time, too! Why can't I get any *obedience* any more, why do you all make things so difficult for me, do you want to kill me, is that it? Come forward, you, what's your name?'

Unwillingly, Naismith floated toward her. 'Naismith,' he told her.

'That's not a name, are you making a joke of me? What is his name, I say, what is this Shefth's name?'

'He does not know his name, Highborn,' said the robot. 'He is to be referred to as "that man".'

'Be quiet!' screamed the fat woman. 'You, are you a Shefth?'

'As you see, Highborn,' said Naismith. A globe of watchers, most of them hugely fat, was beginning to form around them.

'Impertinence! When have I ever had to bear such insults! *Do* you know how to kill a Zug, answer me directly, and mind your manners!'

'I don't know,' said Naismith.

'He is the only Shefth we have, Highborn,' said the baby-pink fat man, bending near.

'Well, I don't like him! Go back and get another one at once, do you hear me, take this one away, I won't have him, I won't!'

'Highborn, there is not enough time—' said the fat man.

'Time, time, don't we manufacture time, how can you be so cruel and thoughtless, don't contradict me, I say, go and get another!'

Two or three of the men around the fat woman exchanged glances.

'Well, what's wrong with you all, are you deaf or paralyzed, why can't I get a simple order obeyed in Mind's name, oh, why are you all ...'

A chime sounded nearby; heads turned. 'One moment,' said the pink man anxiously. 'Highborn, the message.'

The woman fell silent, gaping and blinking. There was a movement in the globe of people as the pink man drifted back. Now Naismith could see a yellow box-shaped machine with a lighted face, suspended in a transparent globe. The chime came again. The pink man tilted himself nearer, staring at the face of the machine. Naismith could see words forming in threads of white light, one, then a gap, two more, another gap ...

'"Danger ... Zug alive ... send Shefth".' The pink man paused, then straightened. He sighed. 'That's all. Almost the same as last time.'

'Well, it's clear enough, isn't it?' the woman screamed. 'Danger, send Shefth – to kill the Zug, that's clear, isn't it, what more do you want?'

'But the words left *out*, Highborn,' the pink man said despairingly.

'Never mind, you're only trying to confuse me! They want a Shefth to kill the Zug – *we* want a Shefth, up there in the future, that's clear, isn't it? Well, then, what's the matter?'

There was motion in the globe of watchers; a hawk-nosed man, leaner than the rest, came plunging through and stopped before the fat woman. Behind him was a gnome in brown and red stripes, one of the scientists. 'Highborn, this man says Prell has been killed in the workrooms!'

'Prell? Killed? Who killed him? Who is Prell?'

'The time-laboratory director, Highborn! His spine was broken, not more than five minutes ago.'

'There is the man who did it!' blurted the gnome suddenly, pointing his finger at Naismith. Heads turned; there was agitated motion in the group.

'He did it? Then kill him, quickly, quickly, you idiots, before he does it to somebody else! What are you waiting for, kill him!' The woman grew yellow-faced and shrunken; her little eyes glistened with fear.

'One moment,' said the hawk-faced man. 'Autos – that man.' Three of the dark, red-lensed machines drifted toward Naismith, taking up positions around him.

'Kill him!' squalled the woman.

'That can be done in a moment, after we ask one or two questions,' said Hawknose. He turned to Naismith. 'Don't make any sudden motion, or the guns will fire. Did you kill Prell?'

'No,' said Naismith. He caught sight of Liss-Yani hovering in the background.

'Who did, then?'

'Uglies,' said Naismith. 'They came into view, killed him, disappeared again.' Sweating, he tried to relax.

'You saw this?'

'Yes.'

'Why didn't you speak of it?'

'No one gave me an opportunity.'

The man's lips quirked in a half-smile. 'Where is that robot?' he asked, turning.

The box drifted up to him; Naismith recognized the red and green arabesques. 'Yes, sir?'

'Is this the man who told you Uglies had killed Prell?'

'Yes, sir.'

'Did you see it happen?'

'No, sir.'

'Did the automatics fire, or did the alarm sound?'

'No, sir. That man said they were out of order, sir.'

'Were they?'

'No, sir.'

The hawk-faced man turned to Naismith again. 'That seems conclusive. Have you anything else to say?'

'Kill him!' screamed the woman again. 'Kill him! Kill him!'

'What about the Zug, Highborn?' ventured the pink man.

'The Zug, I don't care about the Zug...'

'But who will kill it, if *we* kill the Shefth?'

'Get another one,' she muttered. 'Don't bother me with these details, I've told you a million times. I don't want to be bothered, can't you understand that, I only want to be left *alone*—'

'One moment,' said Hawknose. He gestured toward the nearest of the machines. Blackness flapped suddenly toward Naismith.

For a heart-freezing instant, he thought the gun had fired; then he realized he had been enclosed by another of the dark globes. Through it he could hear their voices, but could not make out the words.

Time dragged unendurably. Then, suddenly, the little group broke up; the dark globe vanished.

'Well, that's settled,' said Hawknose agreeably. 'You're to have a reprieve, Shefth. We're going to let you kill a Zug – here, on this side of the Barrier. If you do, well and good. If not—' He shrugged, turned to the gnome beside him.

'Give him some equipment and get the gate ready,' he said. 'A few of you go along and watch – you, you and you. Anyone else want to go? All right, four vehicles, then. See to it.'

As he turned away, there was a babble of voices around Naismith. The gnome had darted away and disappeared; other bright forms were clustering nearer. Naismith caught sight of Liss-Yani, and of a smooth-limbed, athletic man who might have been her brother. Two gorgeous fat men in candy stripes of violet and pink drifted up, chattering excitedly to each other.

With a look of sullen hostility, the gnome reappeared carrying a small bundle of equipment. 'This way.'

As the group followed him, he edged closer to Naismith and muttered, 'You animal, you're going to be clawed up and eaten alive inside half an hour. I'll be watching, and I'll laugh!'

Naismith felt chilled. The holiday mood of the people around him, their laughter and bright faces, suggested that they were about to enjoy some amusing spectacle. *Clawed up and eaten alive* ... Would that amuse them? A cold fury came to drive back his fear. Somehow, somehow he would cheat them of that pleasure.

Darting ahead, the gnome checked at one of the mirror disks. He touched it briefly. The disk cleared: they were looking into a tiny, blue-walled room, on the far wall of which glimmered another silvery disk.

'Go ahead, get in,' said the gnome impatiently.

Naismith entered the chamber slowly, glancing around him. The gnome handed him a clutter of harness and equipment. 'Put these on.'

Naismith examined the objects. There was a pistol-like

weapon in a holster, a helmet with a curious forward-jutting spike, and a complex webwork of plastic straps with metal insets.

'Here, let me show you,' said the man who resembled Liss-Yani, coming forward. 'Rab-Yani is my name. You may call me Rab.' He took the harness from Naismith's hands, deftly looped it around his torso, arms and legs.

'What's this for – to protect me from the Zug?' Naismith demanded.

Rab-Yani gave him an odd look. 'It gives some momentary protection,' he said. 'Nothing short of a force-field will protect you against a Zug, however. What this does principally is to seal off wounds and prevent shock. In that way, you can go on fighting for another few seconds before you lose consciousness.'

Naismith watched grimly as the Entertainer passed the holster strap around his chest. The projecting gun-butt looked familiar; he grasped it, drew it half out of the holster.

Yes, it was the same – the massive, powerful grip and barrel.

'That's your flamer,' said Rab-Yani. 'It projects a spear of intense flame which will cut through even a Zug's hide, if you are close enough. It is good for three shots before it becomes too hot to hold.'

Naismith thought this over in silence. Behind him, the excited voices continued; then the sound faded, and suddenly a ghostly blue bubble floated past him; in it were the two fat men, staring back at him with onion eyes. The bubble passed through the wall ahead and disappeared.

'Now the helmet,' said Rab-Yani, fitting it onto Naismith's head. 'This contact goes here, on your cheekbone. Clench your jaw.'

Naismith did so, and at once a faintly shimmering disk appeared, hanging in front of his face from the spike of the helmet.

'That's for illusions,' Rab-Yani said. 'The Zug may appear in some confusing shape, but look through that, and you will be able to see its real aspect.

Naismith relaxed his jaw; the disk winked out.

'Well, we're ready,' the Entertainer said. Two more ghostly bubbles floated past. In one of them crouched the gnome, who gave Naismith a malevolent glance before he disappeared.

Turning, Naismith saw Rab join Liss-Yani: he floated close to her, she touched the controls of the machine she held, and a blue shadow-sphere formed around them.

The bubble floated nearer: Rab-Yani gestured toward the gateway in the wall ahead, and Naismith saw that it was now open, revealing blue-violet depths.

Feeling very much alone, he took a deep breath and floated through.

The gigantic, deserted corridors of the Old City had a dreamlike familiarity to Naismith: again and again he recognized places he had encountered before, in his dreams and in the machine memory the aliens had given him: but they were all changed, empty, shadowed. Here was a great concourse, on whose elaborate, fluted central stem Naismith remembered seeing a colorful crowd perched, fluttering, coming and going like a flock of tropical birds: now it was an echoing vault.

Later, they drifted along the tops of hundreds of ranked cylindrical shells, each twenty feet wide, in whose purple depths vague, indecipherable shapes could be glimpsed. 'The Shefthi growth cells,' Rab commented, drifting close to his bubble. 'You came out of one of those ... do you remember?'

Naismith shook his head. Part of his mind was aware of the blue bubbles, with their chattering occupants, drifting insubstantially around behind, above him. Another part was listening to what Rab-Yani said. The rest was fiercely alert for danger.

'What about you – did you come out of one of these, too?' he asked abstractedly.

Floating beside Rab in the bubble, Liss-Yani laughed. 'No – then he would have been a Shefth! The gravity in those cells is set at one and seven tenths Earth normal. He would have too many muscles!' She put her arm around Rab with casual affection.

The gnome's bubble darted suddenly forward, disappeared through the solid wall.

'And you abandoned all this, just to get away from the Zugs?' Naismith asked. 'Why?'

'When they mutated, they became very strong and very intelligent. The Old City is full of tunnels and passages, too many ever to flush them all out. That's why you Shefthi were created. We never needed a warrior caste before – not for thousands of years.'

'If they're so intelligent, why not deal with them?'

Rab gave him a surprised look. 'The Zugs are predatory upon man,' he said slowly. 'They eat our flesh, and plant their eggs in our bodies. There are men at this moment, hidden away down here, paralyzed, while Zug larvae grow inside them. Yes, we could deal with the Zugs, but only on their terms. Do you think you would like that, Shefth?'

Naismith said stubbornly, 'But why try to kill them with weapons like this?' He touched the gun at his chest. 'You could be safe inside one of those bubbles, shooting them down with force-rods. They wouldn't have a chance.'

Rab exchanged glances with the girl beside him, then looked around. The other bubbles had spread out; neither was within earshot.

'Listen to me, Shefth,' he said in a low voice. 'Are you really as ignorant of the Zugs as you pretend?'

'I don't remember anything about them,' Naismith said flatly.

'Then you are probably doomed, because Pendell has gone ahead to find one, and it will not be hard. You must realize this: these creatures are the fiercest man-killers in the history of the universe: but they are not mindless animals. If we hunt them with superior weapons, they stay in hiding. That is why you have no armor that will protect you for more than an instant, and no gun more powerful than that one. If you were trained, there would be one chance in two of success; as it is, you will have only a few seconds to kill the Zug before it kills you. It is incredibly fast and agile. It—'

He broke off suddenly as the gnome's bubble reappeared ahead. The expression on the little man's face was one of malicious triumph.

'Quickly,' said Liss-Yani in an urgent voice.

'You must hold your fire until it is almost upon you,' Rab finished tensely. 'It will dodge your first flame and come at you from a different direction. Your only chance it to anticipate that direction, and—'

A scattered chorus of shouts broke out from the bubbles behind them. Tense, hand on his gun, Naismith stared around.

What he saw was nothing more frightening than a small bald man in white robes, who had just entered the corridor from a narrow opening ahead. His pale blue eyes stared across at Naismith without expression; then he turned and was gone.

'Now the Zug will certainly come,' Rab muttered. 'That was a scout.'

'A man?' Naismith asked incredulously. 'There are human beings serving them?'

'I *told* you,' Rab began, then stopped abruptly. From the opening ahead, something else had emerged into view.

Naismith's hand slapped his chest instinctively, came up with the cool metal of the gun, even as his mind registered the incongruity of what he was seeing. The thing that was now hurtling toward him with incredible speed, winged, glittering, was no Zug – it was an angel.

Naismith had an impression of blazing eyes, a manlike face of inhuman beauty, powerful arms outstretched.

In that frozen moment, he was aware of the passengers in the bubbles, all facing around, bright-eyed, intent, like spectators at a boxing match. He saw the gnome's bubble begin to move. Then his jaw clenched, and the view-disk sprang into being in front of his face. The angel disappeared; in its place was a many-legged monster, red-eyed, clawed and hideous.

'Zug!' shouted the voices around him. Then the beast was upon him.

Naismith fired. A spear of flame shot out of the pistol, blue-bright, twenty feet long. The monster wheeled in mid-air, seemed to vanish.

Naismith whirled desperately, knowing as he brought his gun around that he had no chance. He saw the gnome hanging close behind him in his blue bubble, almost close enough to touch.

There was no time for conscious thought: he simply *knew*. The gun fired in his hand: the lance of flame shot out, straight through the gnome's insubstantial body.

A wailing chorus went up. The gnome, unharmed, whirled to look behind him. Then he began to howl with fury.

Drifting in the air, its huge body still writhing, armored tail lashing, the Zug lay with its massive head cut half from its body, and a trail of violet-red blood streaming from the wound.

The spectators in their bubbles began to close in, shouting with excitement. Rab and Liss-Yani were hugging each other.

Naismith felt himself begin to tremble. It was over; he was still alive.

'How did you do it? How did you ever do it?' shouted one of the candy-striped fat men, edging nearer, cheeks shining with pleasure.

'Pendell was too close,' Naismith said with an effort. 'He came up behind me, knowing the Zug would use him for cover.' He took a deep breath, and smiled at the gnome. 'Thank you,' he said.

Pendell flinched as if he had been struck; his face writhed. As laughter burst out around him, he turned and darted away.

The view-disk in front of Naismith's helmet had winked out again. Curious, he turned to look at the Zug: and where the monster had been a moment before, an angel lay slain.

The pale head, half severed, was noble and beautiful; the

eyes stared blindly. The great limbs tensed spasmodically; the sharp tail curled up and then was still.

15

Naismith was dreaming. Part of his mind knew that his body was afloat, curled up in mid-air in the green-walled cubicle; another part was drifting through dream images, memories, distorted and menacing – the pale Zug, more horrible than in life, with fangs and gleaming eyes, looming toward him, while he hung paralyzed, unable to reach for the gun...

Naismith groaned, trying to awaken. The image faded. Now he was wandering through the deserted corridors of the Old City, somehow confused and blurred together with the corridors of the spaceship. The greenish faces of Lall and Churan floated into view; they were dead, their dull eyes turned up.

And a part of his mind, separate from the other two, was watching in fascinated horror as a door trembled, about to open.

The crack widened. In the darkness, something stirred, came into view...

Naismith awoke, with his own hoarse cry echoing in his ears.

His clothing was sweat-sodden; his head ached, and he was trembling all over. A shout echoed in the distance, outside the cubicle. For a moment he wondered if he were still dreaming: then the sound came again. It was a shout of alarm, or fear. Other voices answered it; then came a rolling rumbling avalanche of sound – an explosion!

Naismith gathered himself and shot to the doorway, looked out. A man of the Entertainer caste, armed and helmeted, face intent, went by down the corridor.

'What is happening?' Naismith called after him, but the man was gone.

On the way to the social room, he passed two groups of hurrying automatic guns, their red lenses aglow; the second was accompanied by a robot, which did not respond to his questions. Somewhere, very distant, sounded the rumble of another explosion.

The huge globular hall was filled with motion. People were rushing in all directions, interfering with each other, often colliding. Robots and automatic guns were everywhere. There were a few greenskinned servants, all with the metal collars around their necks, all with wild, stunned expressions. He passed one male greenskin who was arguing or pleading with a stout man in white. The man, who was carrying a viewscreen on which a tiny picture was visible, shifted a few yards away from the servant, not looking at him; the servant followed, still talking, and so they moved jerkily across the hall. Naismith drifted after them and listened.

'... to kill me like this,' the greenskin was saying in a hoarse, indistinct voice. 'Tell them not to do it, please tell them—'

'Leave me alone,' muttered the man, gazing into his viewscreen. He moved away again. Again the servant followed.

'Don't let them kill me, that's all I ask,' he said thickly. 'I'll do anything. I'll be good, I'll never be slow when you call again – just please tell them—'

Without speaking or looking up, the man moved away. The servant fell silent and gazed after him. His heavy face turned blank; then he shuddered, his face darkened, his muddy eyes bulged. With an inarticulate sound, he launched himself through the air, arms outstretched.

He never reached the man in white. In mid-air, his head suddenly dropped, his body went limp. He floated, turning slowly, past the man in white, who did not even glance up.

From the back of the metal collar around the dead greenskin's neck, a thin trickle of blood crept into sight.

Naismith turned, went on his way. Here and there in the huge space, he saw other drifting, greenskinned bodies. One or two were being towed away by sarcophagus robots; the rest were being ignored.

He noticed, too, that the man in white was not the only one with a viewscreen. Almost every member of the ruling caste had one; and where the people clustered thickly, he discovered, they were watching larger screens that hung in the air.

Naismith moved on. Movement flowed around him, voices called in excitement; once he saw an Entertainer with a bloody face being carried past by a robot. But it was all dreamlike, distant.

What was wrong with him? He felt a tension in himself that was slowly, steadily increasing, and it seemed to him that it had been building continuously all this while, ever since that first day in the multiple classroom in Los Angeles. Every step, from the death of Ramsdell, his imprisonment, then Wells' murder . . . traveling forward with the two aliens, the buried spaceship, all the way to the City . . . that tension had been remorselessly growing inside him. He felt as if his body were being physically distended by it, till he must burst if he could not find relief. His forehead was sweating; there was a tremor in his arms. Something inside him . . . that buried mystery, the thing that had taken over in the psychiatrist's office, and again in Prell's laboratory . . . the black secret of his being. . . .

He felt as if the door were about to open, and as if its opening would destroy him.

'Shefth, what's the matter with you?'

He looked up. It was a fat little man in brown and green stripes, gazing at him with anxious eyes. The shrill voice went on, 'Don't you know the Highborn has been asking for you? Where have you been? Come along, hurry!'

Naismith followed toward the center of the hall, where the largest cluster was located. As they made their way slowly through the close-packed, moving bodies, the little man panted back at him, 'Hurry, hurry – she wants you there before it happens!'

'Before what happens?' Naismith asked dully. The pressure inside him was so great that he could scarcely breathe. His head ached, his hands were cold.

'The Barrier!' the little man shrilled. 'They are going to put up the Barrier any minute! Hurry!'

Squeezing his way through the inner ring, Naismith came into view of the fat woman and her entourage, gathered around a row of big circular screens. One showed a view of the time-laboratory workrooms, with a gnome in the foreground – Pendell, or another just like him. The fat woman was screaming hysterically, 'Isn't it ready yet? How soon, then, how soon?'

'A few minutes, Highborn.'

'Why can't you be more specific? A few minutes, a few minutes – how many?'

'By my estimate, not more than five,' said the gnome. His face was strained; he was giving part of his attention to the aristarch, part to a control box he held in his hands.

'But I want to know *exactly*,' the fat woman shrilled. Her eyes were mad in her yellow face. 'Go forward in time and find out, as I asked you to before!'

The hawk-faced man drifted up and said, 'That would pinch out the loop, Highborn. It is contrary to the basic laws of time.'

'Pinch out the loop, pinch out the loop, that's all I hear!' the old woman screamed. 'I'm tired of it, tired of it! How many minutes now?'

'Perhaps three,' said the gnome, tight-lipped.

'Highborn, the trap worked!' said a grime-streaked Entertainer, darting up, his face jubilant. 'The Uglies were destroyed – we have their time vehicle!'

'Good!' said the fat woman, looking momentarily pleased. 'How many does that leave?'

The men beside her turned toward one of the floating screens, in which nothing showed but a scattering of greenish points of light. As Naismith watched, a few winked out, here and there.

The nearest man touched the edge of the screen, peered

at the numbers that appeared at the bottom. 'Seven hundred fifty-three, Highborn,' he said.

'Good! And how many Zugs?'

The group's attention turned to another, similar screen, in which the dots of light glowed sullen red. 'The same as before, Highborn,' said a man. 'Five hundred eighty-seven.'

The old woman snorted with indignation. 'Still so many?' she said. 'Why, I say why?'

'The Barrier will kill them, Highborn,' Hawknose reminded her gently.

'Then *how long* is it till the Barrier?' she demanded.

'Less than one minute,' said the gnome. Drops of sweat stood on his brow.

In his mounting distress, it seemed to Naismith that the whole great gathering had turned sordid and ugly, the colors dulled; even the air he breathed smelled overperfumed and fetid. This was a sorry climax to the drama of the human race, he thought – this pampered oligarchy of piggish little men and women, selfish, ignorant and stupid – less worthy to survive than the Entertainers who amused them, or even the neurasthenic technicians who kept their city functioning. And now there would be no threat to their dominion, for ever and ever ... That, somehow, was the most intolerable idea of all.

'Ready!' the gnome snapped. His eyes gleamed with excitement as he glanced around. Behind him in the darkness, Naismith could see the other technicians floating beside their machines, all with faces upturned toward Pendell.

'Now!' said the gnome harshly, and his fingers touched the control box.

Naismith felt an instant's violent and inexplicable alarm. Something seemed to compress his lungs; a band of pain clamped around his forehead.

Shouts of excitement echoed in his ears. All across the vast space, men and women in gaudy costumes were swirling about each other in rapid motion.

'How many Uglies left?' the old woman cried. 'How many, I say how many?'

'None, Highborn!' a man called triumphantly. In the screen, every green light had winked out.

Glancing across the hall, Naismith saw many drifting greenskinned corpses, but not one living servant.

'And how many Zugs?' called the old woman.

A hush fell. In the second screen, one ruddy light was still burning.

'One,' said the nearest man reluctantly. 'One Zug left alive, Highborn.'

'Fool!' she screamed at Pendell. 'Fool, fool! How could you be so careless? Why didn't your Barrier kill them all?'

'I don't know, Highborn,' the gnome said. His face twitched; he blinked, rubbed his thin arms with his hands. 'In theory it is impossible, but—'

'But there it is!' she shouted. 'Well, what are you going to do? How can we be safe if there's a Zug still alive? Where is that Shefth? I say where is he?'

Several hands thrust Naismith forward. 'Here, Highborn.'

'Well?' she demanded, whirling, her mad eyes staring into his. 'Well? Are you going to kill it? What are you waiting for?'

Naismith tried to speak, and failed. His body was on fire with pain; he could barely see.

'What's the matter with him?' the old woman squalled. 'I say what's the matter?'

Hands probed his body. Dimly he heard the hawk-nosed man's voice: 'Are you ill?'

Naismith managed to nod.

'Look at him, just look!' the old woman shouted. 'What good is he now? Put a death collar on him and be done with it!'

'But the Zug, Highborn!' called an anxious voice. 'Who will kill the Zug?'

'Put the collar on him, I say!' the woman's hysterical voice railed on. 'I can't stand the sight of him. Put the collar on him – kill him, kill him!'

Naismith felt a moment of intolerable tension, then a sudden release. He was afloat in darkness, safe, protected.

The woman's shout seemed to echo from a distance. 'Well, why don't you put the collar on?'

A pause. Another voice answered: 'Highborn, this man is dead.'

16

In the darkness, the being who knew himself as Naismith awakened. Memory returned. He knew where he was and what he was.

He was alive, though the rapidly cooling body in which he lay was not. He could remember, now, with utter clarity, all the things it had been necessary for 'Naismith' to forget.

He remembered killing Wells. Earlier, he remembered standing beside the wreckage of a bomber, and coolly selecting the dog tags of one of its crewmen, the one who most resembled him in age and height: dog tags that read 'NAISMITH, GORDON'.

He remembered stripping the body, carrying it on his shoulders to a ravine, throwing it in and covering it with boulders. . . .

Earlier still, he remembered his first grublike awareness – warmth, protection, motion. He had put out pseudoganglions, first cautiously, then with gathering sureness and skill. He had linked his own nervous system with that of his host, a Shefthi warrior returning belatedly from a Zug hunt.

Then he could see, feel, hear, with his hosts human senses.

He was inside the Shefth: he *was* the Shefth. . . .

With grim satisfaction, he realized that the game was over, the long-maturing plan had been successful. His knowledge of his own kind came only from human sources, but logic alone made it certain that he represented his species' counterblow to the humans' Barrier. Encysted in a human body, his mind radiations mingled with those of a human brain, he alone of all his kind could pass through that Barrier. *He* was the one surviving Zug: he himself was the monster he had been sent to kill.

Now, as his strength returned, he was aware of motion. The host-body was being towed off out of the way, probably by a robot. He waited, tensely, until the motion was arrested and the sounds of voices diminished. It was evident that he had been taken out of the great hall, into some smaller chamber.

He waited again, to make sure, but there was no further movement.

Ever since the host-body died, he had been injecting desiccants into it to harden it and make it brittle along the center line of the torso. Now he streched himself, applied pressure: and the body split. Light came into his prison.

For the first time, he saw with his own eyes; and he was dazzled. The world was so much more brilliant and beautiful than human senses could convey!

Now he saw that he was floating in a small, bare cubicle, among the corpses of dozens of greenskins.

Carefully he drew himself out of the hollow he had made in the body of his host. He felt his limbs and wings stretching in the air, hardening.

A fresh babble of voices came from outside the cubicle. He gripped the empty host-body and drew it quickly to the back of the room, hiding it behind the other floating bodies. A moment later, there was a commotion: a body crashed heavily into the room, followed by another. The first was babbling in a thin, terrified voice. 'No, no, no ...'

He risked a glance. A robot, as he watched, was affixing a death collar to the scrawny neck of a technician. Its task done, the robot turned and floated away. It was carrying a cluster of the metal collars, which jangled faintly as it moved.

The technician, left behind, tugged vainly at his collar. Tears glittered in the little man's eyes. With a choked sound, after a moment, he turned and followed the robot.

The being who called himself Naismith waited grimly. Now that the Shefthi and the greenskins were gone, the City's rulers were evidently making sure of the technicians – perhaps of the Entertainers as well. However that might be, Naismith waited because he had to.

During the first few minutes, he was vulnerable and weak, easy prey for any determined man with a weapon.

At intervals, cautiously, he tested his wings. The curved ribs were hardening, the mebranes drying. He flexed his grasping members, watching the armored segments slide in their casings. Strength and alertness began to flow into his body. Soon—

His thoughts broke off abruptly as another robot entered the chamber. Naismith felt a tug, and saw the greenskinned bodies around him bob and wheel, as they followed the robot out into the corridor.

Naismith went along, caught in the same web of force. Outside, he saw that his small group of bodies was being joined to a much larger one. All the greenskinned corpses evidently, were being brought together for disposal. Naismith could have broken free of the weak attraction that held him, but he ran less chance of detection in staying where he was. Besides, if his idea of his whereabouts was correct, the procession was headed where he wanted to go.

Other groups of bodies were added as they went, but always at the head of the procession, and it was not until they crossed a large spherical hall that anyone noticed Naismith.

'Look – a Zug, isn't it?' an effete voice remarked. 'How frightening, even dead as it is!'

'Yes, and imagine that we aren't even seeing its true form,' another voice replied. The sound faded as the procession moved on. 'If we had a viewer to look at it with—' A pause. 'But, Willot, what is a dead Zug doing *here, in the New City*?'

Naismith waited no longer. With a surge of his wings, he was out of the cluster of bodies, darting straight across the hall toward the nearest doorway.

Shouts echoed behind him as he gathered speed. Ahead, a little group of gorgeously dressed fat men blundered squarely into his path. He burst through them like a rocket, sending them flying with bruised limbs and broken bones.

Then he was at the doorway, thinking his destination. He dove through, into the workrooms of the technicians.

Here everything was confusion – machines unattended and adrift, unidentifiable instruments floating in clusters. A few technicians were visible, most of them wearing the death collars. Of the few who were still without them, one was being pursued, shrieking, by a robot.

The dim memories of his last sleep were now clear. Naismith remembered stealing out of the cubicle, going to the workrooms, capturing and subduing one of the technicians. He had put a mind helmet on the little man, had forced out of him the one secret he wanted to know.

Now he headed directly for one small doorway, half-hidden behind floating machines. He opened it with a thought, dived in.

There was a gnome before him in the narrow, blind tube. He had the rear panel already open, and was fingering the controls. He turned a snarling face as Naismith entered; then his eyes widened, his face paled.

Naismith killed him with one blow, pushed his body aside, and turned his attention to the control board.

Here, carefully concealed and guarded, was the central control system for all the automatic devices that made life possible in the City – air generators, synthesizers, automatic weapons, robots.

Naismith examined the control disks carefully. Some had the death symbol on them, meaning their settings could not be altered without killing the operator – an underling would have to be sacrificed for each such adjustment. These were the controls for the force-fields which made up the walls of the New City; the precaution was understandable.

Others, of a slightly different color, also bore the death symbol, but in these cases it was a bluff, and Naismith touched them without hesitation. He turned off all the automatic weapons in the City, neutralized the robots, and opened the gateways between the Old and New Cities. Then, working more slowly, he opened the panel and altered the thought signals required to approach the control board. Now only he could make any further changes in its settings.

He was hungry, so he made a light snack from the food he found in the corridor. Then, at his leisure, he went back the way he had come and began the tour of the City.

Everywhere, the Lenlu Din gawked at him with pasty faces, all silent, all shaking. Those nearest the doorways fled in a panic when they saw him enter: the rest did not even try to escape, but only hung where they were, passive, staring.

He paused to examine his reflection in the silvery disk of a mirror. It was strange, and yet perfectly natural, to look at himself and see this pale, unearthly figure, with its blazing eyes in the inhuman mask of the face. He flexed his great arms, and the smaller grasping members; then the tail, watching the sharp sting emerge.

He moved on, giving new orders to the robots as he went. In the social room he came upon a little group of fat men frantically at work upon an instrument he recognized.

They scattered as he approached, and he read the message they had been trying to send into the past: 'DANGER – ONE ZUG ALIVE. DO NOT SEND SHEFTH'. The machine was glowing, the message incomplete. He turned it off, and went on his way.

He was here, nothing they could do could alter that. That had been obvious from the beginning: but let them try.

The vast concourses and galleries of the New City absorbed his attention; he was beginning to catalogue the treasures of his new domain, a task that would occupy many months. Yet the silent throngs, the glittering color, the miles of records and information capsules, did not please him as they should. After a long time he realized what the trouble was. It was the phantom personality of the man, Naismith. It was oppressive, as if he were wearing an invisible overcoat. Irritably he tried to shrug it off, but it stayed.

Now that he was aware of it, the feeling was more annoying than ever. He stopped and floated still, appalled. Every thought, every feeling that Naismith had had during the months their minds were linked together was recorded in his brain. It was not merely that he remembered Naismith: he *was* Naismith. He was a member of the race of conquerors; and he was also a man.

He made a violent mental effort to throw off that phantom mind, but the thing clung to him stubbornly, like the ghost of an amputated limb. It was no use telling himself that Naismith was dead. Naismith's ghost was in his mind – no, not even a ghost; his living personality.

He whirled in sudden anger, and the fat little people scattered around him. Were *these* the rulers of Earth's ultimate City, the inheritors of four hundred thousands years of human evolution? These puffed little parasites, selfish, neurotic and cruel?

Their race produced some great men, Naismith's voice said soberly in his mind.

There are none among these! he answered. Nor will they ever produce any, if they live a million years.

Not under your rule.

And if I had left them to themselves, what then – would they have done any better?

No, there is no hope for them, nor perhaps even for the technicians. But there is hope for the Entertainers.

Pride stiffened his body. They are my property.

They are human beings.

In doubt and confusion, he turned to the nearest robot, a sarcophagus-shape with geometric figures inscribed in red on a gold and silver ground. 'Tell me briefly, what is a human being?'

The robot whirred, hummed. 'A human being,' it said, 'is a potentiality.'

After a moment, he gestured. The robot bowed and drifted away.

The Entertainers deserve their chance, Naismith's voice said.

No.

He turned as another robot floated up: he recognized it as one he had sent into the Old City on an errand.

'Lord, I found no Masters alive, but I have taken eggs from their bodies as you ordered. They are under the care of the technicians in the biological laboratories.'

He made a sign of dismissal and the robot went away. He went on with his tour of inspection. Everywhere, the eyes of the little fat people stared at him in dull misery.

Woe to the vanquished, said a voice in his brain: was it his own, or Naismith's?

With a sense of panic, he discovered that he could not tell the difference. The two were one.

He was all triumph and mastery; yet he was all commiseration, all regret.

Give them their lives, and their chance, said the voice.

Where?

Where but on Earth?

Naismith hung frozen for a moment, remembering the sea of grass, under the cloud-dotted sky.

A little man in white drifted up. 'Master, are there any orders?'

'Yes. Find me the Entertainers Liss and Rab.' As the human bobbed his head and darted off, Naismith beckoned the nearest robot. 'Bring me a vehicle.'

Still, when the robot had gone, he hung in the air, oblivious to the color and movement around him, astonished by the purpose that was in his mind. Could a Zug feel this passion of mercy, and remain a Zug?

The robot came first with the control box, then the Entertainers, looking frightened and desperate.

Naismith took the control box. 'Come near, and don't be afraid,' he said to the Entertainers. 'We are going to Earth.'

'To Earth? I don't understand,' said Liss-Yani.

'Are you going to exile us there?' Rab burst out. He turned to the girl. 'Let him do it,' he said fiercely. 'It's better than staying here to be food for him.'

Liss-Yani's face paled. After a moment, she stepped nearer, and Rab followed. Naismith touched the controls. The blue-tinted bubble of force sprang up around them; the hall drifted away. They passed through one partition, then another ... then a third, and they were in space, under the cold majesty of the stars.

They stood on the grassy plain just at dawn, when the greenish-blue sky to eastward was lit with yellow fires along the horizon, and the sun bulged up red as a blood-orange above the mountains.

Naismith switched off the bubble. The two Entertainers looked at him without expression, then turned and began to walk away through the wet grass. After a moment they linked hands.

'Wait,' Naismith called after them. They turned. 'How far does the influence of this machine extend?'

'About half a mile,' the girl said dully.

'Then if I take it farther away than that – or better, if I remove it in time – you will die?'

'You know we will.'

'Then watch.' Naismith touched the controls, forming the bubble. He depressed and rotated the time control gently.

The two silent figures vanished; the plain writhed, darkened, glowed with sunlight, darkened again. Touching it more gently, Naismith turned the control the other way. The same sequence unrolled in reverse, like a film strip run backward.

The two figures appeared once more, then a third – Naismith himself, wings busy as he hovered in air, his grasping members holding the machine.

Invisible in the bubble, he watched himself leave. He saw the two Entertainers stiffen, saw them clutch each other. After a moment he saw them separate, open their eyes, look around in wonder.

Still he waited, until they dared to walk a few steps into the grass, calling to each other, breathing deep. Dawn was diffusing half the sky; across the plain, birdsong echoed.

Naismith lowered the bubble, brought it into phase and turned it off. The two humans did not even see him.

'Liss – Rab!' he called.

They turned, with incredulous faces. 'It didn't kill us!' said Liss-Yani. 'Is this *real*?'

'It is real,' he told her.

'But then—' she whispered, and fell silent.

'They said that you Zugs made the illusion,' said Rab.

'They also told you we were hideous monsters,' Naismith replied drily. 'Which is easier – to make an illusion you can see with your own eyes, or to make one that can only be seen through a "viewer"?'

They stared at him. 'This is your true form?' Liss-Yani ventured.

'It is my only form.'

'And all this is real?'

Naismith did not reply. They were a pretty pair, he was thinking, especially the female; it would be interesting to breed them and see— He checked himself. Was that the Zug's thought, or the man's?

It was neither, he realized, but a blend . . . and how curious to think that this detached pleasure, half cool, half warm, was possible only to the mythological creature he had become. . . .

'But why would they do this?' Rab asked.

'Tell me, when you left the City on their errands, did you ever think of staying on Earth?'

'Yes, often,' said Liss, her eyes glinting.

'Why didn't you do so?'

'If we had stayed in the past, that would have changed history, changed the City – so it was impossible – it would have pinched out the loop.'

'And why didn't you settle *here*, in your own present?'

The two looked at each other. 'Because they made us think it was a wasteland,' Rab said.

Naismith inclined his head. 'We will go back to the City now,' he said. 'You will tell the other Entertainers, gather them all together. I will give you vehicles, tools, records, everything you need.'

They came toward him slowly. 'But why are you doing this?' Liss asked.

'You would not understand,' said Naismith.

... In truth, he hardly understood himself. But as he moved through the glittering throng in the great hall, listening to the music and the voices, seeing the respectful looks on the faces of the Lenlu Din when they glanced his way, it seemed to Naismith that somehow, through accident and willfulness, he had woven himself precisely and symmetrically into the grand design.

Always, he thought, the universe tended to strike a balance between two excesses: long life and short, intelligence and mindlessness, mercy and cruelty. The tapestry unrolled, and there was never an end to it.

'Lord,' said a robot, drifting up, 'the last of the Lenlu Din are being processed now in the gold chamber. In one hour they will all have been treated, as you ordered.'

Naismith dismissed it, and watched it float off among the idle pleasure-seekers. He was pleasantly hungry: in half an hour it would be time to eat. After all, this way was best. In the old days, a Zug would have leaped upon his victim and devoured it on the spot. Now ...

A few hundred yards away, from the midst of a large group, he heard the screeching of the old woman, the Highborn, hysterical and angry as ever. Other voices were soothing her. All was normal, all was for the best in this best of worlds.

Naismith drifted over; the gaily dressed little people parted respectfully to let him through. Even the mad old woman interrupted her screeching to bob her head.

'Highborn,' said Naismith, 'have you forgotten that you are about to retire for extended meditation?'

'I am? Am I?' she said uncertainly. 'When am I going?'

'Almost immediately,' Naismith told her gently, and beckoned to a passing robot. 'Show the Highborn to her chambers.'

'But won't that be unpleasant?' she asked, letting herself be led away.

'You will not mind it at all,' Naismith promised her, and

floated off in another direction.

Three fat little men, arms linked, drifted across his path with respectful glances. To them, he was no monster, but a revered counsellor and guide. The absence of the Entertainers did not strike them as odd: Drugged and hypnotized, they had forgotten there had ever been such a caste, or any other state of things.

They were cattle.

Was this mercy? Then a Zug could be merciful. Was it cruelty? Then there was cruelty in a man....

The game, Naismith realized now, was not over. The pattern was still unfolding, in this small and unimportant corner of the universe of stars.

Here, in the closed world of the City, he tasted triumph – dominion was his. Yet it was good to know that down there on Earth, the human species was still free, still evolving in its pattern.

It was pleasant to think that in a thousand years, or ten thousand, Zug and Man might meet again, and this time blend their powers into something greater. It would take that long, or longer; Naismith and his kind could afford to wait.

For God is not born in a day.

Also in Hamlyn Paperbacks

Robert Silverberg

THE SEED OF EARTH

The computer had chosen them – a small cross-section of humanity to serve Mankind's Destiny. Out of seven billion people on Earth mechanical chance had selected them as involuntary colonists on an unknown planet. In seven days they would be on their way, on a sink-or-swim mission to a lonely world beyond the limits of the Solar System.

It was a summons each had privately dreaded, yet always been prepared for. But no one had prepared them for the vicious attacks of sinister aliens.

Also in Hamlyn Paperbacks

Brian M. Stableford

THE FLORIANS

Once a colony ship had left Earth it could not be recalled or even contacted. The fate of these vessels and their passengers remained a tantalizing mystery to those who stayed at home.

The mission of the scientific recontact ship *Daedalus* was to go out there and discover what happened – and to help the colonists if their developing worlds were in difficulties.

This is the account of the first flight of the *Daedalus* and its crew of seven. On the world of the Florians they did indeed find a planet in trouble – but the inhabitants refused to admit it.

Also in Hamlyn Paperbacks

Henry Kuttner

FURY

The Earth is long since dead, blasted in a self-sustaining chain reaction. Human survivors settled on Venus have organized themselves into a static, class-ridden society living in huge citadels buried beneath the Venusian seas.

The rulers are Immortals, genetic mutations who live a thousand years or more. Their subjects are the ordinary people with normal life-spans.

Sam Reed's insane father had him mutilated as a baby so that he doesn't realize he's an Immortal until he reaches the age of eighty. Then he goes looking for revenge . . .